"The Idea That I Would Ever Be Dumb Enough To Fall For You Is Pretty Funny."

"Dumb enough?"

"Yes, dumb enough. Let me count the ways." She held up one hand and began ticking off fingers. "First, you're a grouch in the morning. You leave newspapers lying around everywhere. You date a woman once and then never call back. You're a big baby when you're sick."

Brandon had heard enough. He placed the file on the chair in front of her desk and stalked closer. He brushed against her, then slipped his hand around her nape and urged her closer.

She moaned. "What are you doing?"

"What do you think I'm doing?"

"I'm not sure."

"I am."

And then he kissed her.

Dear Reader,

I grew up in California and always loved visiting the Napa Valley wine country. So it didn't take much arm-twisting for me to choose those romantic, grapevine-studded hills and valleys as the backdrop for Brandon Duke's story.

Confident, handsome Brandon is the third of the Duke men to face his comeuppance from his mother, Sally Duke. The most determined of the brothers to fend off his mom's matchmaking maneuverings, Brandon is nevertheless taken by complete surprise when his bespectacled, sensible secretary, Kelly, returns from vacation looking absolutely stunning. But then he finds out her true reason for getting a fashion makeover—and that's when he really gets into trouble!

I've always enjoyed the forbidden fantasy of the boss and secretary love affair. I suppose you might attribute it to the fact that I worked as a legal secretary for many years. But trust me on this: I never worked for such a gorgeous boss as Brandon Duke! I would've remembered!

I hope you love reading Brandon and Kelly's story as much as I loved writing it. Please stop by my website at www.katecarlisle.com and let me know. While there, you'll find pictures and links to some fantasy resorts I imagine the Duke men might've owned, as well as background stories and fun facts about me and my books.

Happy reading!

Kate

KATE CARLISLE

HOW TO SEDUCE A BILLIONAIRE

Harlequin® Desire

Recycling programs for this product may not exist in your area.

ISBN-13: 978-0-373-73117-6

HOW TO SEDUCE A BILLIONAIRE

Printed in U.S.A.

KATE CARLISLE

New York Times bestselling author Kate Carlisle was born and raised by the beach in Southern California. After more than twenty years in television production, Kate turned to writing the types of mysteries and romance novels she always loved to read. She still lives by the beach in Southern California with her husband, and when they're not taking long walks in the sand or cooking or reading or painting or taking bookbinding classes or trying to learn a new language, they're traveling the world, visiting family and friends in the strangest places. Kate loves to hear from readers. Visit her website at www.katecarlisle.com.

Champagne, chocolate and many thanks
go to my brilliant editor, Stacy Boyd, for helping me
give Brandon and Kelly's romance a truly happy ending.

One

"Memo to self: Cancel all employee vacations," Brandon Duke muttered as he reached for his coffee cup and realized it was empty. Yet another reminder that his invaluable assistant, Kelly Meredith, was still away on vacation. She'd been gone for the past two weeks, and that was fourteen days too long as far as he was concerned.

It wasn't like Brandon couldn't get his own cup of coffee. He wasn't that lame. It was just that Kelly always beat him to it, showing up with a piping hot refill at the right time, every time. She was a dynamo in every other way, too. Clients loved her. Spreadsheets didn't intimidate her. And she was an excellent judge of character, something he'd recognized early on. That was a quality worth its weight in gold and he'd taken advantage of it from the start by having Kelly accompany him to various business meetings all over the country.

Brandon's own instincts were spot on when it came

to judging a potential business partner or the motives of a competitor, but Kelly was a strong backup. Even his brothers had gotten into the habit of having Kelly vet new hires and solve problems in other departments. They called her the miracle worker, for good reason. If there was a thankless job that needed handling, Kelly grabbed it with both hands and worked her magic. Everything ran more smoothly because of her.

Taking advantage of the early morning quiet in the still empty office suite, Brandon grabbed a legal pad and began to scribble notes for a meeting with his brothers later today. Now that the Mansion at Silverado Trail, the Dukes' newest resort in Napa Valley and the jewel in the crown of the Duke hotel empire, was about to celebrate its grand opening, it was time to focus his energies on new properties and new challenges.

Reading what he'd written, he was reminded of another reason he needed his assistant to come back from vacation: she could decipher his handwriting.

In the middle of bullet-pointing several options for a takeover bid on a small chain of luxury hotels along the picturesque Oregon coast, Brandon checked his calendar. Every hour of the day was filled with appointments, conference calls and deadlines, many of them connected to the grand opening celebration. Good thing his assistant would be back today, and about damn time. The temp replacement had been competent, but Kelly was the only one who could handle the myriad pressures and scheduling conflicts involved in the upcoming festivities.

And speaking of pressures, his brother's wife was about to pop out a baby soon. This would be Mom's first grandkid, and you would've thought no other child had ever been born. Talk about a major celebration. But what in the world was Brandon supposed to buy the kid? Season tickets on the 49ers' fifty-yard line he could swing, but otherwise, he was clueless. Didn't matter. Kelly would know the perfect gift to buy and she'd probably wrap it, too.

Brandon heard rustling and the sound of drawers opening just outside his partly opened door.

"Good morning, Brandon," a cheery voice called out.

"About time you got back, Kelly," he said with relief. "Come see me after you've had a chance to settle in."

"You bet. I'll just make a pot of coffee first."

Brandon checked his watch. Sure enough, she was fifteen minutes early, one more indication that she was an ideal employee who deserved all the perks the job offered. But he still planned to outlaw vacations from now on.

"Ah, it's good to be back," Kelly murmured as she powered up her computer. Hard to believe, but she'd actually missed Brandon Duke while she was gone. The sound of his deep voice gave her a little thrill she attributed to the fact that she loved her job.

She stashed her tote bag and purse in the credenza behind her desk and quickly made coffee. Her hand shook as she filled the pot with water at the small kitchen kiosk across from her office and she forced herself to relax. She really was happy to be back at the job she loved, so why was she so nervous?

Okay, she'd made a few changes while on vacation, but nobody would notice, right? Nobody ever noticed anything about her except for her savvy business sense and can-do attitude, and that was just the way she wanted it. So if she happened to be wearing a dress today instead of one of her usual pantsuits, who would care? The fact that she'd never worn a dress to the office before wouldn't stand out to anyone here. Even if today's dress was a beautiful dark gray knit that buttoned up the front and clung subtly to her curves. And that was just fine and dandy.

And if she'd finally changed over to contact lenses, so what? She'd been wearing the same boring eyeglasses for the past five years. Change was a good thing.

"Kelly," Brandon called from his office. "Bring the Dream Coast file with you when you come in, will you?"

"Be right there."

The familiar sound of Brandon Duke's voice made Kelly smile. He should've intimidated her from day one. At six feet four inches tall, he towered over her, and she knew for a fact that he was rock-solid muscle underneath his designer suits. She knew, because she'd run into him more than once at the hotel gym and seen him in shorts and a T-shirt. A former NFL quarterback bench-pressing ridiculously heavy barbells was quite a sight. Sometimes, while watching him, she found it hard to breathe steadily, but she chalked up those moments to spending too much time on the treadmill.

She chuckled at the thought of some of her girlfriends, who'd told her they would kill for a chance to see the stunningly handsome Brandon Duke working out in gym shorts. Luckily for Kelly, she'd never been tempted by her boss.

Yes, he was gorgeous, almost unbelievably so, but to Kelly, having a great job meant a lot more than having a brief, meaningless affair with some superstar athlete. And yes, an affair with Brandon Duke would never be anything but brief and meaningless. She'd seen firsthand the women who lined up to date him, and she'd seen them flicked off without a backward glance within a couple of weeks. It wasn't pretty, and she never wanted to find herself in that line. Not that she would qualify to stand in that line, but—

"What are you thinking?" she whispered to herself.

She'd never thought of her boss in those terms before and she wouldn't start now. Shaking her head in disgust, she had to wonder if maybe she'd taken too many days off.

As the coffeepot filled, Kelly took a moment to glance out the wide bay window and felt both proud and lucky to be here in this job. Who wouldn't want to work on a hilltop in the heart of Napa Valley, overlooking lush fields of grapevines as far as the eye could see?

Brandon and his small corporate staff had been working on-site at the Mansion at Silverado Trail for the past four months. They would stay here another month or so, until the resort was up and running and the grape harvest was over. Then they would all relocate back to Duke headquarters in Dunsmuir Bay.

By then, Kelly's plan would be complete, and her life would settle down to normal. But until then, she would simply have to remind herself to relax and breathe.

"Do you hear me, self? Just relax," she murmured as she ran her hands over her dress to smooth away any wrinkles, then filled two large mugs with hot coffee. "Breathe."

She stopped at her desk to drop off her own mug and pick up a short stack of mail, then pushed her boss's door fully open.

"Good morning, Brandon," she said breezily, and placed the mail on his desk.

"Morning, Kelly," he said, as he wrote rapidly on a legal pad. "Great to have you back."

"Thank you, it's nice to be back." She placed his mug on his blotter. "Coffee for you."

"Thanks," he said absently, still writing. After a moment, he reached for his coffee and looked up. His eyes widened as he cautiously put the cup down. "Kelly?"

"Yes?" She gazed at him, then blinked. "Oh, sorry. You wanted the Dream Coast file. I'll be right back with it."

"Kelly?" His voice sounded strained.

She stopped and turned. "Yes, Brandon?"

He was staring at her in...disbelief? Shock? Horror? Oh, dear. Not a good sign. And the longer he stared, the more nervous she became.

"Oh, come on," she said. "I don't look bad enough to have stunned you into speechlessness." She fiddled with her dress collar as she felt heat moving up her neck and settling into her cheeks. No need to be embarrassed, she scolded herself.

"But, what did you do to..." His voice trailed off as he continued to stare at her face.

"Oh, you mean the contact lenses? Yeah. It was time for a change. Be right back with the file."

"Kelly." His tone was demanding.

She turned again. He was still staring, this time at her hair. With a sigh, she brushed a strand back from her cheek. "I had it lightened and shaped. No big deal." Then she waved him off and rushed to find the file.

Great. If Brandon was any example, people would be staring at her as if she were an alien. How was she supposed to relax and breathe and put her plan into action under those circumstances, darn it?

As she anxiously rifled through the file drawer, she heard the distinctive sound of Brandon's leather executive chair rolling back from his desk. Seconds later, he was standing in the doorway. Still staring.

"Kelly?" he said again.

She stared up at him from the files. "Why do you keep saying my name?"

"Just making sure it's you."

"Well, it is, so cut it out," she told him, then found what she was looking for. "Ah, here's that file."

"What did you do?"

"You asked me that already."

"And I'm still waiting for an answer."

Her shoulders drooped for a split second, then she straightened. There was no reason to feel self-conscious, especially not with Brandon. He'd given her glowing reviews and generous raises. He respected and admired her ability to work hard and solve problems. He was her employer, not her overlord, for goodness sake. "I got a little makeover."

"Little?"

She raised one shoulder in a casual shrug. "That's right. I lost a few pounds, got a haircut, some contact lenses. No big deal."

"It is from where I'm standing. You don't even look like you."

"Of course I look like me." She wasn't about to mention the week spent at the pricey spa or the private etiquette and speech lessons. He would think she'd gone insane. Maybe she had. She'd always been levelheaded, and rational to the point of being called a nerd back in college. Now she wasn't sure what they would call her.

"But you're wearing a dress," he said accusingly.

She looked down, then back at him. "Why, yes, I am. Is that a problem?"

It was his turn to look discomfited as he took a step back. "No. God, no. No problem at all. You look great. It's just that…" Scrubbing his jaw with his knuckles, he searched for the words. "You don't wear dresses."

He'd noticed? Color her surprised. With a resolute smile, she said, "I do now."

"I guess so," he said, searching her face, still looking doubtful. "Well, like I said, you look great. Really great."

"Thank you," she said, still smiling. "I feel great."

"Yeah. That's great." He nodded, then gritted his teeth and exhaled heavily.

If everything was *great,* why was he scowling?

"Oh!" she said, feeling ridiculous as she thrust the thick manila folder at him. "Here's the Dream Coast file."

His hand grazed hers as the file passed between them and she felt a buzz of awareness all the way up her arm.

Brandon's frown lines deepened. "Thanks."

"Sure thing."

He walked back into his office, then turned. "It's great to have you back."

And that was how many *greats* so far? she wondered.

"Thank you," she said. "And I'll have the month-end sales figures calculated for you in twenty minutes."

He closed the door and she sagged down into her chair. Grabbing her own cup of coffee, she took a big gulp. "Oh yeah, it's *great* to be back."

Brandon tossed the Dream Coast file onto his desk and continued walking across the plush office until he reached the floor-to-ceiling window that lined one long wall. He and his team were working out of the owner's suite on the penthouse level of the Mansion at Silverado Trail, and he never grew tired of the view. Normally, when he gazed out at the gently sloping hills of chardonnay grapevines, he relished the pride he felt when he saw such visible symbols of his family's success.

A hot air balloon drifted silently in the sky overhead and birds skittered from tree to tree across the hills. But he ignored all of it as he caught the barest whiff of flowers and spice drifting in the air. He wasn't used to his assistant wearing perfume, or maybe he'd never noticed that she did, but for the first time ever, the arresting scent conjured up visions of a cool hotel room and a hot blonde. Naked. Wrapped in sheets. Under him.

Kelly. He could still smell her. Damn it.

He'd made a fool of himself just now, gaping at her as though she were a juicy steak and he were a starved puppy. Hell, he hadn't even been able to speak. He'd sounded like a damn parrot, repeating her name over and over. But he would lay the blame for that solely at her feet. She'd succeeded in shocking the hell out of him and that never happened to Brandon Duke.

A makeover? He shook his head as he paced the length of the wall of glass. Who could fathom a woman's mind? Kelly didn't need a makeover. She'd been fine the way she was. All business, completely professional, smart, discreet. Never a distraction.

Brandon didn't like distractions in the workplace. In his office, it was all business, all the time. After ten years in the spotlight of the NFL, he was all too aware that distractions ruined your game. You took your eye off the ball and the next thing you knew, you were buried in a pile of tough, ugly defensive ends who would just as soon see you dead.

Brandon splayed one hand on the plate glass window. Talk about a distraction. Who knew his competent assistant had those amazing curves and world-class legs hidden beneath the boxy pantsuits she'd worn every day? And those eyes, so big and blue a man could get lost in them?

Most disturbing of all, she seemed to be wearing some kind of new, glossy lipstick. It had to be new, otherwise he would've noticed her incredibly sexy, bee-stung lips long before today. But he was noticing now. He'd almost spilled his coffee noticing.

Her new dress clung to every curve of her lush body. Curves he'd never known existed before. Even though he saw her in the hotel gym regularly, she always exercised in a big T-shirt and sweatpants. Who knew she'd been hiding a body like that under all those layers of sweaty workout clothes? She'd clearly been working here under false pretenses all this time.

"Now you just sound ridiculous," he groused. But who could blame him? His sedate, hard-working assistant was simply gorgeous. It was such a betrayal.

And what the hell had happened a minute ago when her hand touched his? He thought he'd felt something sizzling inside him. It had to be his imagination, but recalling that sensation of skin against skin caused his groin to leap to attention. He smacked the wall in disgust.

"Change is good," he grumbled sarcastically and he sat back down at his desk. No, change *wasn't* good. Not when he was used to Kelly's nondescript hair and the way she'd always worn it pulled back in a sensible ponytail or bun. Now it was the color of rich honey tumbling across her shoulders and down her back. It was the sort of color and style that begged a man to run his hands through the lustrous strands as he eased her down to feast on those luscious lips.

His body continued to stir to life and he squelched the feeling by slapping the file folder open and riffling through the papers to find the document he needed. It was useless.

"This is unacceptable." He refused to lose the careful sense of order and decorum he had always maintained in the workplace. The job was too demanding and Kelly was too important a part of his staff to allow her to suddenly become a distraction. Or more aptly, an *attraction*.

It was time to nip this in the bud. He reached across his desk and pressed the intercom button on his phone. "Kelly, please come in here."

"Be right there," she said briskly. Seven seconds later, she walked into his office carrying a notepad.

"Sit down," he said, standing up to pace some more. He didn't quite trust himself with taking another glance at her legs. Damn it, this just was not going to work. "We need to talk."

"What's wrong?" she asked in alarm.

"Look, we've always been honest with each other, haven't we?"

"Yes," she said carefully.

"I trust you completely, as you well know."

"I know, and I feel the same, Brandon."

"Good," he said, unsure of his next move. "Good."

Now what? He'd never been at a loss for words before. He glanced at her, then had to look away. How and when had she become so beautiful? He knew women. He loved women. And they loved him. Some might even say he had a sixth sense when it came to women. So why hadn't he known Kelly was this attractive? Was he blind?

"Brandon," she said slowly. "Are you unhappy with my work?"

"What? No."

"Did Jane do an okay job while I was gone?"

"Yeah, she was fine. That's not the problem."

"Oh good, because I would hate to—"

"Look, Kelly," he interrupted, tired of this cat and mouse game. "Did something happen to you on your vacation?"

She was taken aback. "No, why would you think—"

"Then what's with this makeover thing?" he blurted out. "Why'd you do it?"

"That's what you called me in here for?"

"Yeah." And he wouldn't go into how ridiculous he felt

for bringing it up, but he had to know. "Why do you think you have to get all dolled up to—"

Her eyes narrowed. "All dolled up?"

"Well, yeah. You know, all made up and…hell."

"There's something wrong in trying to look my best?"

"That's not what I said."

"Did I overdo it somehow? I mean, the makeup counter woman showed me what to do, but I'm new at this. I'm still practicing." She lifted her face to gaze at him and her lips seemed to glisten as they caught the light. "Tell the truth. Is my makeup too much?"

"God, no, it's just right." Too damn right, he thought, but didn't say.

"Now you're being nice, but I don't believe you. The way you looked at me when I came in this morning…"

"What? No." *Oh, crap,* he thought. She wasn't going to cry, was she? She'd never cried before.

"I thought I could do it. Other women do it, for heaven's sake, why shouldn't I?" She jumped up from the chair. It was her turn to pace as she pounded her fist into her palm. "I thought I was being subtle. Do I look like a fool?"

"No, you—"

"You can be honest."

"I'm being—"

"This was a crazy idea to begin with," she muttered and leaned back against the wall with a sigh. "I can figure out complex mathematical calculations in my head, but I don't know the first thing about seduction."

Seduction? Something hit him low in the solar plexus and he wasn't sure of his next move.

"This is so embarrassing," she moaned.

"No, it's not," he said, silently hoping he'd come up with something profound to say. He had nothing.

"What am I supposed to do now? I've only got a week

left to…oh, God." She covered her eyes for a moment, then stared up at the ceiling. Finally, she folded her arms across her chest and tapped one toe of her shiny new heels against the carpet. "How could I be so stupid?"

He walked up to her and grabbed her by the shoulders. "Stop that. You're one of the smartest people I know."

She glared up at him, her plump lips pouty now. "Maybe in business, but never in romance."

Okay, romance and seduction were definitely on her mind. And now he realized they were on his mind, too. The question was, why? In all the years he'd known Kelly, Brandon had never once heard her mention a name connected to any romantic interest. And now, all of a sudden, she was making herself over to attract some guy? Just who was she thinking of seducing? Did Brandon know the guy? Was he good enough for Kelly?

Brandon paused to carefully word his next question. "Who are you trying to seduce?"

Frowning now, she stared at her fingernails. "Roger. My old boyfriend. But I should've known it wouldn't work."

Roger? Who the hell was Roger? Brandon had to admit that the part of him that should have been relieved to hear she wasn't out to seduce *him* was surprisingly disappointed. Not that he would ever allow anything to happen between them. But still, who the hell was she talking about?

"Who's Roger?" he asked aloud.

"I just told you, he's my old boyfriend. His name is Roger Hempstead." She stepped away from Brandon's grip and moved back to her chair. "We broke up a few years ago and I haven't seen him since."

"How long ago did you break up?"

"It's been almost five years."

He made a quick calculation. "But that's about how long you've been working here."

"That's right." She leaned one elbow on the armrest and looked up at him with a valiant smile. "After Roger and I broke up, I couldn't stand living in the same small town where everyone I knew could dissect my every word and movement. I decided to relocate as far away from home as possible, so I looked for jobs in California and found this one."

"I'm glad you did, but it must've been quite a breakup."

"It wasn't fun," she said carefully, "but I've moved on."

"Have you?"

"Yes, of course." She nodded her head resolutely. "But then, last month I found out that Roger's company booked their corporate retreat here at the Mansion. He'll be here next week." She took a deep breath and exhaled. "And I wanted to knock his socks off."

"Ah, I see." And he did, sort of. Resting his hip on the edge of his desk, he said, "If it's any consolation, I can pretty much guarantee you'll knock his socks off."

She gazed at him skeptically. "You're just saying that to be nice."

"I'm not that nice. Trust me."

Her lips twisted into a frown. "I do. Usually."

"I never lie, remember?"

"True, you don't typically lie. To me, anyway," she allowed.

He chuckled. "So it's been about five years since you broke up with this Roger character, and now you want to make an impression."

She nodded with determination. "I really, really do."

"You will. I promise."

"Thanks." Her brief smile faded. "But I don't know what I'm doing. I'm fine at business, but the world of romance is beyond me."

"Tell me what I can do to help."

Kelly regarded him with interest. "You mean it?"

"Sure." He was willing to do almost anything to get things back on track. If Kelly felt secure, she'd be able to do her work and stop worrying about this clown Roger. Then, once Roger was gone, she'd go back to behaving like the Kelly he was comfortable with. His universe would once more be in alignment.

"That would be wonderful," she said with enthusiasm. "I could really use advice from someone like you."

"Someone like me?"

She smiled and he was struck again by how beautiful she was. Damn, how blind had he been all these years?

"It's just that the two of you are so much alike," she said. "You and Roger, I mean. It would really help to get your perspective on things."

"What do you mean, we're alike?"

"I mean, both of you are strong and handsome and arrogant and ruthless and, you know, type A all the way."

Huh. That was accurate enough, although he'd always thought he was fairly laid-back compared to his two brothers. He did appreciate the strong and handsome part of her description, though.

Kelly had stopped to ponder what she'd just said, then added softly, "Wow, no wonder Roger didn't think I was enough for him."

Brandon bristled. "*Enough* for him?"

She sighed. "You know what I mean. I wasn't attractive enough for him."

"What makes you say that?"

"He told me so when he broke up with me."

For some reason, Brandon felt an irresistible urge to pulverize something. Like Roger's face. "You're kidding."

"No," she said wryly. "I'm really not. But you saw what I looked like before the makeover, Brandon. Plain, wholesome, unremarkable. Not exactly supermodel material."

A twinge of guilt pinged inside him as he realized that was exactly how he'd always felt about her. But he'd considered that a good thing. Now he was just glad he'd never mentioned it out loud.

"But I understood where Roger was coming from," she continued. "He is very special, after all."

"Special? He sounds like a jackass."

She tried to stifle a giggle but didn't quite succeed. "Oh, he is, but he can't help it. His family has a very strong influence on him. His mother's ancestors came over on the *Mayflower,* you know."

"Members of the crew, were they?" Shaking his head, he said, "Listen, Kelly, do you want me to have him killed? Because I know someone who knows someone who could—"

Kelly laughed. "That's a sweet offer, but no. I just want to make him regret what he said when he broke things off, that's all."

He studied her for several moments. "He hurt you."

She shook her head. "No, no, he told me the truth and I have to be grateful for that."

"Grateful? Why?"

She smiled tightly. "Because he helped me see things more clearly."

"What kinds of things?" Brandon asked warily.

"My own shortcomings."

Once again, his fists were itching to punch something. Roger's stomach, maybe, since he'd already mentally broken the jerk's nose.

She smiled brightly. "So that's why I've decided to get him back."

"What? Get him back?" Why in the world would she

want that scumbag back? Hell, Brandon didn't even know Roger and he already hated him.

"Yes." She spread her arms out. "And that explains the makeover."

And with that, she made a show of checking her watch, effectively ending the conversation. Probably a good idea.

"So," she said, changing the subject, "do you want me to order lunch from catering?"

He wasn't finished talking about this, but clearly Kelly needed a time out. So he'd let it go. For now.

"Yeah, that would be great. I'll have the steak sandwich."

"Sounds good. I'll call it in."

He leaned forward in his chair. "Listen, Kelly, if you need any help or advice, anything at all, you'll come to me. Promise?"

"Really? You mean it?"

"Absolutely."

She studied his face as if she were weighing the depth of his sincerity. "You're sure?"

"I wouldn't have offered if I wasn't."

She seemed to carry on a short debate with herself, then said, "Okay, there is one tiny thing you could help me with. If you wouldn't mind."

"You name it," he said, reaching for his coffee mug.

"I'll be right back." She rushed out to her desk and was back in less than twenty seconds, holding a shopping bag from a well-known and expensive lingerie shop. Taking a deep, fortifying breath, she pulled some wispy scraps of sheer material from the bag and dangled them for him to see.

"Which do you like better, the black thong or the red panties?"

Two

He choked on his coffee.

Dismayed, Kelly ran around and pounded his back. "Are you okay?"

"Fine," he managed to say. "I'm fine." He'd be even better once she backed off and her curvaceous breasts were no longer rubbing against his arm. He was only human, for God's sake. And hard as granite.

He'd been tackled by some of the biggest linebackers in football history, but nothing had ever rendered him apoplectic before now. As he took a deep breath and let it out, the thought entered his mind that maybe she was trying to kill him. Could Roger have treated her so badly that she was going to take it out on every man she knew?

It wasn't enough that she'd changed the playing field with her hot new look, but now she was shoving her panties at him. Didn't she know that those little scraps of silk would be forever imprinted on his fragile male psyche?

Now he would be forced to spend the next millennium imagining her in that black thong. Was she really that clueless?

"I didn't mean to shock you," she said. "But you said you would help."

"Didn't shock me," he insisted, his voice sounding as if a frog had taken up residence in his throat. "Coffee went down wrong. Just…give me a minute."

She finally moved back to her side of the desk and quickly shoved the bits of lace into the shopping bag.

"They'll work just fine," he said softly, not trusting his voice yet.

Her eyes glittered with hope. "Really?"

"Believe it," he said with a nod. "Any normal guy would be grateful to see you in either pair."

"You mean it?" Her eyes cleared and she smiled. "Thank you, Brandon. Oh, and I apologize again for springing them on you."

"No problem."

"To make this work, I really need to know what guys consider sexy." She frowned, then admitted, "Roger never thought I was."

"Never thought you were what?"

"Sexy."

Brandon sat forward in his chair. "Does Roger have some kind of learning disability or something?"

She laughed. "Thanks for that. I'll go order lunch now."

"Good idea," he said, thankful his voice had returned to full volume. "Oh, and Kelly?"

She stopped at the door. "Yes?"

"Go with the black thong."

Later that afternoon, Brandon hung up the phone from a two-hour teleconference with his brothers and their lawyer.

"That guy never stops talking," he said, shaking his head at the sheer immensity of the lawyer's convoluted vocabulary.

"I was thinking you must pay him by the word," Kelly said, flexing her fingers. She had taken notes during the entire meeting and now she stood and stretched her arms. The movement caused the knit fabric of her dress to stretch so tightly across her perfect round breasts that Brandon had to look the other way to stifle the first stages of another rock-hard erection.

"I'm getting more coffee," she said. "Would you like some?"

"No, thanks. Will you have a chance to type up your notes and analysis this afternoon?"

"Definitely. I'll get right on them."

"I appreciate it."

She closed the door and Brandon gritted his teeth. He needed Kelly to rethink this new wardrobe situation if he was going to survive the week. Hell, even her ankles were causing him palpitations. There was something about those high heels she was wearing that did awesome things to every inch of her legs.

An hour later, after the rest of his team had gone home, he walked out to Kelly's area to find a property file and caught her pouting at herself in her compact mirror.

"Oh." She blinked in surprise and quickly slapped the mirror closed and threw it in her drawer.

He rested one hand on the doorjamb. "I know I'm going to be sorry I asked, but what were you doing?"

"Nothing. What do you need? A file? Which one? I'll get it." She jumped up and pulled the top file drawer open.

"See, now you're just raising my curiosity level," he said, "so you might as well tell me."

She clenched her teeth together irately. "Fine. Roger

complained about the way I kissed, so I was practicing in the mirror. There. Are you happy?"

He shook his head. "Roger is a complete idiot. Why do you care what he thinks?"

She glared at him. "I told you, I want to get him back."

"Yeah, that's what I don't get." Disgusted with the subject of Roger, he moved to the file drawer and began to sift through the folders himself. "Where's the new Montclair Pavilion file?"

"I've got it right here." She picked up a thin folder and handed it to him. She looked so dejected, he couldn't help but feel sorry for teasing her.

"Look, I'm sure you kiss like a goddess," he said. "So stop worrying about what Roger thinks."

"I just wish I could practice on something besides a mirror," she said gloomily.

"Yeah," he agreed absently as he thumbed through the file. "It usually works better to go with a real-life target who'll actually kiss you back."

She shot him a hopeful look. "I don't suppose you'd be willing to help me out with that."

He glowered at her. "Get real, Kelly."

"What do you mean?" Realization dawned slowly. "Oh! No, no! I didn't mean for *you* to kiss—oh, dear. I would never want *you* to…well, this isn't going to come out right, no matter how I say it."

"So just say it."

"Okay. I wasn't talking about *you* kissing me." She sat on the edge of her desk. "But the thing is, I've made a list of potential, um…participants. So I was thinking maybe you could help by looking it over and making some suggestions?"

"You have a list?" Why was he surprised? Kelly made

lists for everything. It was just one of the ways she stayed so organized.

"Of course I have a list." She jumped up, ran around the desk and pulled a pad and pen out of her drawer. "I'm good at making lists."

"Let me get this straight," he said, absently slapping the file folder against his pants leg. "You've made a list of men you're thinking of approaching to ask for help with—what? Kissing lessons?"

She flipped a page over and studied it. "That's right."

"But I'm not on the list?" he asked warily.

"What? No, absolutely not." She shook her head as she held up her hand in a pledge. "Of course you're not on the list. You're my boss."

"Good. As long as we've got that settled." He should've felt nothing but relief. So why was he getting more annoyed by the minute? She considered him good enough to judge her damn panties but not good enough to kiss?

Okay, that might be the most ridiculous thought he'd had all day. This entire situation was getting out of hand. With a heavy exhalation of breath, he shoved away his own ludicrous reactions and tried to empathize with Kelly's bizarre quandary.

"So who's on the list?" he asked, almost afraid to hear her answers.

She glanced up. "What do you think about Jean Pierre?"

"The hotel chef?" She couldn't be serious.

"He's French," she explained. "They invented the sport, right?"

"No way in hell. Not Jean Pierre. You'd probably start an international incident. Absolutely not."

"Okay, okay." She crossed Jean Pierre's name off her list. "What about Jeremy?"

"The guy who mows the lawns?"

"He's a landscape designer," she said pointedly. "Practically an artist. He might know a thing or two about the art of *l'amour*."

"He's gay."

"Really? Why don't I know these things?" She blew out a frustrated breath as she drew a line through Jeremy's name. "Nicholas the winemaker? He's German, right? He might be—"

"Let me see that list." He snatched the pad from her and gazed at the names. "Paulo, the cabana boy?"

"He's cute," she insisted, a little too desperately.

"Forget it. Who's Rocco?"

"One of the limo drivers."

"Which one?"

"The big guy with the—"

"Never mind." He shook his head. "No."

"But—"

"No," he said, handing the list back. "Throw that away. I don't want you going around kissing the staff, for God's sake."

"Fine." Glaring at Brandon, she ripped the page out, crumpled it up and tossed it in the waste bin. "I suppose you're right. It might send the wrong message."

"You think?" he said, his voice tinged with sarcasm.

She folded her arms tightly across her chest, which only served to emphasize her world-class breasts, damn it.

"So who can I ask for help?" she wondered, leaning her hip against her desk. "I've got a full week before Roger gets here. I could do a lot of practicing in that time. Do you have any friends you could recommend?"

"No."

"Too bad." She pursed her lips in thought. "Maybe there's someone in town who—"

"Not a good idea," he said in a tone that cut off all

discussion. *Not a good idea?* Talk about an understatement. Hell, it was one of the worst ideas Brandon had ever heard. He didn't want her kissing the staff *or* any poor, unsuspecting Napa Valley residents. All he needed was to have the locals talking about the crazy kissing woman from the Mansion on Silverado Trail.

But he could tell by the tension building along Kelly's soft jawline that she was determined to carry out this cockeyed plan of hers. And if she went behind his back and enlisted one of the pool attendants…

Brandon stared at those pouty, glossy lips and realized the only man who could help her improve her kissing technique was him. Mainly because he suddenly couldn't stand the thought of her kissing anyone else.

"Fine," he said brusquely. "I'll help you."

She pushed away from the desk. "But you're not on the list."

"Doesn't matter. I'm going to help you myself because I don't want you scaring away the staff."

She placed her hands on her hips and tilted her head at him. "I know you meant that in the nicest way."

"Sorry. Yes." He shook his head as if to erase the comment. "Of course I did."

She continued staring at him. "I don't think it's a good idea."

"It's the only way I'll know for sure that you're not getting into trouble around here."

"I won't get into trouble."

"I know, because I'll be the one helping you."

Inhaling a deep breath, Kelly let it out slowly, then seemed to brace herself for impact. "Okay. I appreciate this, Brandon." She took a hesitant step toward him, but he held up his hand to stop her.

"Wait. We need to set some ground rules first."

"Ground rules? Why?"

"Because there's no way I'm having you fall for me."

"Fall for you?" She blinked, then began to laugh. "Are you kidding?"

"Something funny?" he asked, insulted.

"Yes," she said, giggling like a schoolgirl. "The idea that I would ever be dumb enough to fall for you is pretty funny."

"*Dumb* enough?"

"Yes, dumb enough. Let me count the ways." She held up one hand and began ticking off fingers. "You're a grouch in the morning. You leave newspapers lying around everywhere. You date a woman once and then never call back. You're a big baby when you're sick."

"Wait a minute," he protested.

But she was on a roll now and seemed to be enjoying herself. "And all your weird superstitions left over from when you played in the NFL? My gosh, wearing the same socks for every game was bad enough, but I also heard that you ate only sardines and blueberries the night before every game. Do you still do that before big negotiations? Who does that?"

Brandon had heard enough. He placed the file on the chair in front of her desk and stalked closer. "The socks were washed between games."

"Oh, really?"

"Yeah, really." He brushed against her, then slipped his hand around her nape and urged her closer. "And sardines and blueberries are both excellent sources of omega-three fatty acids."

"Fascinating," she whispered, as she stared wide-eyed at him.

"Helps the brain function better," he added as he caressed her cheek.

"G-good to know." She sounded wary now, probably smart of her.

He bent to kiss her neck, then murmured in her ear, "The quarterback's the brains of the team, did you know that?"

She moaned. "What are you doing?"

"What do you think I'm doing?"

"I'm not sure."

"I am." And he kissed her. She tasted as sweet and hot as he somehow knew she would. Even more so. He had to work to keep the contact light and simple, because it wouldn't do to get carried away. But that didn't stop him from wishing he could lay her down on the desk, run his hands up her thighs, spread her legs and bury himself inside her.

He had to stop. This was wrong in too many ways to count. If he stepped away from her right now, they could both forget this kiss ever happened.

Then she groaned in surrender and he knew she wanted the same things he did. And he was helpless to stop. He used his tongue to gently pry her lips open, plunging inside her sexy mouth. Her tongue met his in a sensual play of thrust and parry.

He wanted to cup her breasts and flick his thumbs across her peaked nipples, but that was a sure road to madness. So with every ounce of will inside him, he forced himself to end the kiss, reluctantly pulling himself away from her warmth.

"Oh," she whispered, licking her lips as she slowly opened her eyes.

Brandon's insides clenched at the sight of her pink tongue tasting him on her mouth.

"Oh, that was good," she said with a note of surprise. "That was really good."

"Yeah," he said, brooding. "It was."

"I liked it a lot."

So did he, but he remained silent. Otherwise, he might've been tempted to follow through on his desire to have her naked under him. But that would never happen and right now, he needed to regain some degree of control over whatever strange emotions were still churning inside him.

"Roger never kissed like that," she said, watching him thoughtfully.

"Did I mention the guy was an idiot?" he muttered.

"No wonder he didn't think I was sexy," she reasoned. "It's because he didn't make me *feel* sexy."

"I rest my case."

"But *you* did," she declared and smiled up at him. "And now…wow. You know, I really think Roger was the problem, not me. But I can't be sure."

"Yeah, you can," he said gruffly. "Roger was the problem. End of story."

She touched his arm. "Thank you, Brandon."

"You're welcome." He started to head for his office, still trying to steady his breathing.

"Wait," she said.

He turned and looked at her. A slight line of concern marred the smooth surface of her forehead. Her lips were pink and tender and about the sexiest thing he'd ever seen. The fact that he wanted more than anything to kiss her again, made him forge ahead into his office.

"I think I could get really good at this and blow Roger's mind, but I need to practice," she said, following him. She had her notepad in hand again, probably hoping she could make another damn list of all the different ways they could kiss each other. If she only knew.

"Not a good idea," he said, sliding the Montclair file into his briefcase.

"But you said that before and it turned out to be a really good idea."

He pierced her with a look. "No more practicing. Ground rules, remember?"

"I remember, don't worry." After scrutinizing him for a moment, she nodded her agreement. "Okay, I guess you're right."

"I know I'm right," he said, and snapped his briefcase closed.

"Thank you for your help," she said. "It was wonderful. On a purely educational level, I mean."

"You're welcome," he said and led the way out of his office. "Now let's call it a night."

"Oh, I'm going to stay for a while," she said, flipping to a clean page, all business now. "I need to make some notes while everything is still fresh in my mind. I'll need to remember everything later."

"You're going to make notes on that kiss?"

"Yes, for future reference." She'd already begun scribbling what looked like mathematical calculations. "If I write everything down—what you did and what I felt, I'll be able to recall each sensation the next time, and I'll know I'm doing it right."

"The next time," he echoed hazily.

"Yes. I tend to remember tactile experiences more clearly if I make a record of it immediately. Then later, I'll study my notes in anticipation of the next occurrence." She beamed at him. "I'm quite confident I can achieve an exponential jump in my skill level and understanding."

"Really?"

"It makes perfect sense on paper."

"On paper. Good."

Tapping her pen against the pad, she murmured, half to herself, "Of course, an actual kiss would give me a lot more insight...."

She looked up and studied Brandon closely. He wasn't liking the look in her eyes. "Don't even think about it."

"Think about what?" she asked, her eyelashes fluttering innocently. If she were any other woman, Brandon would know she was playing a dangerous game of seduction. But this was Kelly, who didn't seem to have a clue about feminine wiles and whose every emotion was evident on her face.

That made it Brandon's responsibility to set her straight.

"Forget it, Kelly. I am not going to kiss you again."

"Oh, I know," she murmured, her moist, glimmering lips pursed in thought.

He lost all memory of what they were talking about. He only knew that right now, his throbbing body parts wanted to put those lips of hers to the best use possible. Maybe after that, he would be able to carry on an intelligent conversation with her.

In the meantime, however, it appeared that he had created a monster.

Three

"I am not going to kiss you again."

Every time Kelly played the words over in her head, she could feel her cheeks heat up in embarrassment. And since she was incapable of putting a halt to the mental words and images, she wouldn't be surprised if, any minute now, her head spontaneously combusted.

"So stop thinking about it," she demanded aloud as she popped a frozen dinner in the microwave oven and slammed the door shut. Now she had four minutes with nothing to do but wait. And think. And remember. She glanced around her comfortable mini-suite with its corner kitchen nook and figured she could use the time to straighten up, but there was nothing out of place. Her room was pristine, as usual.

The Mansion had a world-class housekeeping service and even though Kelly was part of the corporate staff, the housekeepers kindly insisted on stopping by every day to clean and straighten up and make sure everything was perfectly comfortable for her.

So, lucky her, she had plenty of time to dwell on all those damning thoughts that wouldn't stop circling through her mind.

"The fact that you practically begged your boss to kiss you," she berated herself, "in the office, in broad daylight, wasn't bad enough. No, you also had to dangle your panties in his face. So classy. And why couldn't you keep that silly list of kissing candidates to yourself?"

A small sigh escaped as she slid miserably onto the stool at her kitchen counter. Reaching for the bottle of sparkling water she'd opened, she filled her glass and took a sip. And pondered her next move.

There were a few ways she could remedy the situation. One was to go in tomorrow morning and simply apologize to Brandon. She could explain, somewhat truthfully, that she'd ingested nothing but spa cuisine for ten days straight and it had left her brain incapable of clear thought.

He probably wouldn't believe that story since everyone in the entire company knew that Kelly's mind was a steel trap. She could recall the minor details of a telephone conference from three years ago or the specifications of a particular construction job from months back. She had the dates of every birthday, anniversary and important occasion in Brandon's life memorized, along with phone numbers, credit card accounts and travel preferences for him and every member of his family.

There was no way he'd believe she'd suddenly lost the ability to think straight. So her only other solution was to simply move away, somewhere remote, like Duluth, leaving no forwarding address. She was fairly certain Brandon's memory of the outlandish panty-dangling incident would fade within months, a year at the most.

"Oh, God." She leaned her elbows on the counter and buried her face in her hands. The fact that Brandon had obligingly recommended the black thong really didn't help matters right now.

The microwave buzzed and she removed her small dinner. She was proud of herself for continuing to eat lighter portions since leaving the spa, but she could feel a serious ice cream binge coming on.

It was because of the kiss.

She'd vowed not to think about it and had been semisuccessful, deliberately switching tracks whenever her train of thought veered too close to the memory of Brandon's touch, the feel of his mouth on hers. But now, just for a moment or two, she let herself go and thought about it.

She'd never experienced anything like it. It was just one kiss, but she'd felt more passion and excitement in those few seconds than she'd known in the entire two years and seven months she'd dated Roger.

Now, she closed her eyes and gave in to temptation, reliving the exquisite pressure of Brandon's hands, the warm smoothness of his mouth...

After a moment, her eyes flashed open and she stared down at her rapidly cooling dinner. She'd completely lost her appetite. For dinner, anyway.

"You need to snap out of it, right now," she reprimanded herself. Brandon Duke was her employer. Her job was important to her. She couldn't afford to get dreamy-eyed and moony about the man who signed her paychecks. Especially not *that* man.

Once upon a time, Kelly had envisioned a fairy-tale romance and a happily-ever-after with Roger. He had been her handsome prince and she'd considered herself the luckiest girl in the world. But her prince had turned out to be a frog, and not very charming at all. He'd made promises he never intended to keep and had busted her dream of love and marriage flat. The breakup had not been pretty and Kelly had to admit she hadn't handled it well.

Before she met Roger, she had been upbeat and open to every possibility. She knew she was smart and reasonably attractive, knew she wanted to fall in love, get married and have children some day. But after Roger dumped her so cruelly, she'd felt broken, cynical, awkward and unsure of herself, especially around men. She had lost her confidence and she couldn't think about dating for a long time after the breakup.

Ironically, working in the office with Brandon had been the best antidote for her fears and insecurities. He'd made it clear early on that he considered her an indispensible member of his team. He relied on her intelligence and organizational skills to help him run his projects.

Her self-confidence blossomed and grew until she finally decided she was ready to start dating again. She still wanted to fall in love, get married and raise a family some day. And the only way to achieve that goal was to find the right man.

Being her organized self, she began by calling on her friends and coworkers. Then she'd compiled a list of online dating services as well as a number of local organizations she could join and activities in which she could participate in hopes of meeting eligible men.

She was convinced that she was ready to hit the dating scene—until the day she saw Roger's name on the hotel's upcoming conference list. Her throat tightened and her stomach churned. She couldn't catch her breath. The old insecurities rushed back with a vengeance. That's when she realized she would never be able to love another man until she came to terms with Roger and the damage she'd allowed him to inflict on her life.

If that meant confrontation, then so be it. The only problem with confronting Roger was that his ego was so overblown, he might get defensive and lash out at her. She wasn't sure she could endure another unpleasant war of words with him. But how else could she get around his ego? she wondered. And in that moment, Kelly had devised her life-saving plan.

If she could somehow lure Roger back, then reject him, it would help her recapture some of her old optimism and enjoyment of life. She would be free to move forward and love again. In other words, she would get her mojo back.

She also knew for a fact that Roger wouldn't be hurt by her rejection. Thank goodness, because Kelly could never hurt him on purpose, no matter how unkind he'd been to her. No, the fact was, Roger's ego was much too healthy to allow himself to be wounded by a woman. He would brush off the insult as easily as he would a speck of lint on one of his impeccably tailored suits.

As far as Kelly was concerned, Roger could make up any story he wanted to about why she'd refused him. The point was, *she* would be healed and ready to live again, to open her heart to the possibility of finding love and happiness. Right now, that was all that mattered.

The makeover would certainly help her cause. Kissing lessons couldn't hurt, either, especially from a master of the art. And that brought her back to her current predicament.

"Brandon," she said aloud, moving her fork around on her plate.

The problem was, she wasn't sure she had the experience to lure Roger in after just one kiss from Brandon, even though it had been a potent one, for sure. That's why, on the one hand, she wished she could continue learning the secrets of kissing from Brandon. On the other hand, she knew better. He was her boss! How many times did she have to remind herself? And worse than that—if anything could be worse—was that Brandon could jeopardize her plans for Roger's payback. After all, if Brandon continued to help her with her kissing, it might lead to something more. Kissing often did.

It was useless to deny that she was susceptible. All she had to do was think back to a few hours earlier when Brandon had kissed her. If he'd wanted to take things further, she would've gone right along with him. That's how good his kiss had been.

"Okay, fine, the man can kiss." She tossed her fork on the plate and stood, too antsy to eat.

Even if he kissed her again and it led to something more, she would never be so stupid as to fall for Brandon Duke.

She strode around the room, picking up her jacket and hanging it in the small closet, then sorting through her clothes for tomorrow's outfit.

Yes, she'd laughed at his ground rules earlier that day, but now that she'd kissed him, was she still willing to guarantee that she could remain resistant to his charms?

"Yes," she said firmly, and shoved the closet door shut. She wasn't a complete dummy. She knew Brandon's reputation with women, knew his habit of dating one woman for a brief period of time, then moving on to the next. It would be insane for any woman to expect Brandon Duke to reciprocate her tender feelings. So why would Kelly ever fall for him? She simply wouldn't.

Brandon wasn't the "settle down and get married" kind of guy Kelly wanted to meet and fall in love with. He didn't fit in with her life plan at all.

"And that makes him perfect for *this* plan," she said, as comprehension dawned. Since she would never fall for

him, Brandon Duke was the perfect man to teach her how
to kiss!

Now, if she could just convince him to continue helping
her. After all, look how much she'd learned with just one
try. Her eyes were now opened to the fact that Roger had
been the problem all along. It was obvious now. He had
never kissed her the way Brandon had kissed her. She
would've remembered.

"Oh yes," she said with another sigh as she forced
herself to take another bite of her dinner. She would've
remembered a kiss like that.

So how could she convince her boss to let her practice
her kissing with him some more? Roger would be here next
week so it wasn't as if he would be forced to keep kissing
her forever. It would only be for a few days. She needed
to make it clear that lessons in romance and seduction
would be all she needed. The more skilled she became at
romance and seduction, the better her chances would be
of putting Roger in his place.

Brandon could appreciate that, right?

Still, it was a dilemma. Brandon was her boss. If she
was smart—and she *was*—she'd just forget about Brandon
and use her own best instincts to attract Roger.

What instincts? she wondered, and grimaced. When it
came to romance, she had none!

As she took another bite of chicken and rice, she realized
there had to be a website somewhere with instructions she
could follow. There was a website for everything else, so
why not seduction?

Oh, but it would be so much better to learn from a
real live expert. And Brandon was indeed an expert. She
couldn't help thinking that if mere kissing had given her
this much perspective into her problems with Roger, then
having sex with Brandon would be absolutely revelatory.

"What?" She jumped off her chair and wrapped her arms around herself. Where had that thought come from?

"You stop thinking about that right now," she admonished herself as she grabbed her plate and glass and carried them to the sink. "You'll just embarrass yourself." *Again.*

But now that she'd thought it, she couldn't get the image out of her mind. What in the world would happen if she and Brandon ever had sex?

"Oh, no," she said, gasping. What if they had sex and she found out she really *was* bad at it? How could she face Brandon at work? She would have to quit.

But wait. What if she was really *good* at it? Would he think she'd been lying about her lack of experience? Would he assume she'd been having sex all along, with every guy in town? How could she face him at work? She would have to quit.

And oh, dear Lord. What if Brandon was no good at sex? Would she have to lie and tell him it was wonderful? He was her boss, after all. She couldn't exactly tell him he was a loser in bed. She would have to quit.

She moaned and took another sip of water.

"Okay, that's it," she said, as she tapped her fingers on the counter anxiously. "Just forget the whole thing."

This whole kissing thing was too much to think about. She had to figure out some other way to deal with Roger. She would explain to Brandon tomorrow that she'd been wrong. He would have to forgive her. And she was certain that he would. After all, before today, she'd never done anything to cause her employer the least bit of consternation. Tomorrow, after she explained to Brandon that her brief lapse into lunacy was over, everything would be fine. They'd go back to normal. She would assure Brandon that he would never have to worry about inappropriate behavior from her again.

And a year from now, she would look back and be able to laugh over this momentary ripple in her otherwise unblemished record.

The doorbell chimed and she jumped.

Checking her wristwatch, she wondered if it might be Housekeeping at the door. She'd asked them not to stop by with those yummy evening chocolates anymore. But tonight, maybe she'd take one. Anything to provide a diversion from her disconcerting thoughts. She ran to open the door and her resolutions of a moment ago flitted away.

"Brandon," she whispered.

"We need to talk."

Brandon stared at Kelly and could no longer remember why he'd thought it would be a good idea to come by her room.

After a long run around the hotel grounds after work, then another brief conference call with his brothers to finalize arrangements for their family's arrival to attend the resort's grand opening, followed by a quick taste of the chef's latest creations for the harvest festival menu, Brandon had retired to his suite to watch Dallas eviscerate Denver on TV. But he hadn't been able to concentrate on the football game, and that was a first.

He blamed it on Kelly.

The fact was, he couldn't get her out of his mind. Not in a sexual way, he hastened to tell himself, despite the vivid memory of her warm mouth and sweet tongue and an explicit picture of exactly what he'd like to do with… but he wasn't going to go there. No way. Not with Kelly. Not in this lifetime.

In the first place, she worked for him. How big a fool would he be if he jeopardized his working relationship with the best assistant he'd ever had? And even if he was willing to overlook that little fact, Kelly just wasn't his type. She wasn't sophisticated and worldly like the women he usually dated. She wasn't the kind of woman Brandon would ever think of calling on the spur of the moment for a night on the town, followed by a rousing round of sex, followed by no commitment to call again.

No, Kelly was more like the girl next door, the one who was meant to find a nice guy and get married. As far as Brandon was concerned, she might as well have worn a banner that said Hands Off. And he would be wise to heed that invisible warning.

He'd had some pretty awful role models early in his childhood, before Sally Duke adopted him. He'd seen all the ways people could hurt each other in the name of love and marriage, so he wasn't about to go that route. With that in mind, he had decided not to touch Kelly again.

But she'd looked so pensive and uncertain when he'd left the office earlier this evening. He'd never seen Kelly less than one hundred percent confident in herself and her abilities, so this change in attitude worried him.

And then there was that kiss. Which he wasn't going to think about again, damn it.

So why was he standing here at her door, holding a bottle of wine? Oh, yeah.

"We need to talk," he repeated. He'd used the same stupid line in the office much earlier today. It sounded somehow lamer now, even if it was the truth. When she stepped aside, he strolled into her mini-suite. "I hope I'm not interrupting your dinner."

"No, I'm finished," she said, and rushed to dispose of the remnants.

He held out the bottle of wine, a Duke Vineyards pinot noir. "Will you have a glass of this if I open it?"

She stared at the bottle, then up at him. "Sure. I'll find an opener."

He could tell she was nervous as she rattled around in one of the kitchen drawers. And why shouldn't she be? It wasn't every day a woman kissed her employer. And it wasn't every night that said employer showed up at her hotel room carrying a bottle of wine. He just hoped she wouldn't get the wrong idea. All he wanted to do was clear the air so their working relationship could go back to being as exceptional as it had been before the kiss. It was a simple problem and it wouldn't take him long to explain his feelings, but he had to admit that a quick glass of wine would probably help them both relax.

"Here you go," she said, and handed him a corkscrew.

"Glasses?"

"Oh." She swallowed anxiously. "Right."

As he worked to remove the cork, he took a moment to study his longtime assistant—and wondered how he'd ever thought he'd be able to relax in her hotel room.

She wore cutoff shorts and a T-shirt, an outfit that a jury of his peers would consider thoroughly appropriate for spending a balmy night alone in her room. But as she reached for the wineglasses on the second shelf of the cupboard, he watched her T-shirt inch up to reveal the leanness of her stomach. On her tiptoes now, her shorts stretched just enough to show the soft, pale skin above her tan line where the curve of her bottom met her perfectly toned thighs.

"Here you go," she said, placing two glasses on the counter.

Brandon let go of the breath he hadn't realized he was

holding. "Thanks." He took his time pouring wine into the glasses and handed her one. "Kelly, I—"

"Look, Brandon—"

"Sorry. What were you going to say?"

She blinked, then said in a rush, "No, you go first."

"Fine. I just think—"

"Okay, I'll go first." She glanced briefly toward the ceiling as if she were looking for guidance from above. Brandon watched her chest move up and down as she inhaled, then exhaled. She was clearly edgy. She picked up her wineglass and took a gulp, paced a few steps back and forth across the small kitchen, then stopped and met his gaze, her face a mask of regret.

"I want to apologize for the way I behaved today," she said. "I don't know what got into me. I've been going crazy ever since I learned that Roger would be coming here and I guess I…I lost my head. I'm mortified about what happened. I just hope you'll accept my apology and trust that it'll never happen again."

She looked exhausted when she finished and he felt a twinge of sympathy for her.

"Why don't we sit down?" he said, and he led the way to the cozy sitting area of the mini-suite. They each sat at one end of the small couch, leaving barely two feet of space between them.

He should've been relieved that she'd apologized, but for some unfathomable reason, it didn't sit well with him. "So what, exactly, will never happen again?"

She opened her mouth, then closed it. Frowning, she placed her wineglass down on the end table and shifted against the plush sofa cushions until she was facing him more directly. "You know what I'm talking about."

"Tell me."

"Fine." She exhaled heavily and Brandon was once

again mesmerized by the movement of her breasts. "I backed you into a corner. I practically propositioned you." With a groan of disgust, she lifted her arms and waved them for emphasis. "I threw myself at you." She shot him a quick glance. "Figuratively speaking, of course."

"Of course," he said cautiously.

"I left you no choice but to kiss me, Brandon. It was horrible of me." She grabbed her wineglass. "Don't get me wrong, I appreciate what you did. It was wonderful, really. It was so…well, anyway, you helped me confirm a few important things I'd been confused about. But it was still wrong of me to ask it of you, and I'm sorry. I took complete advantage of you."

"Did you?" He stifled a grin. She didn't honestly think any woman had ever taken advantage of him, did she?

"Yes." She pressed two fingers against her eyelids as though she were getting a headache. "I practically begged you to kiss me."

"Well, you didn't exactly beg." Now Brandon had to smile. He was starting to enjoy this. "But go on."

"I'll understand if you can't forgive me, but I hope you will. All I can do is promise it will absolutely never happen again."

"Never?"

"Never, I swear. In fact, if you could just wipe the entire experience from your memory that would be very helpful."

"You're saying I should just forget it ever happened."

"Exactly! I would be so grateful. You know I've never been a problem employee, so if you could just take this day off the books, I promise it'll never happen again."

He rubbed his jaw, considering. "You've always been above reproach."

"I like to think so," she said, clearly relieved. "Honestly, it was just some kind of momentary aberration. We can chalk it up to vacation-induced insanity or something."

"Or something," he murmured.

Beaming, she said, "You've been really understanding. Thank you so much." She picked up her wineglass and took another sip. "I'm so glad we had this little talk. I feel so much better."

"That's what I'm here for."

She gazed at him, her smile tentative. "I was afraid you came here tonight to fire me."

The words stopped him. "I would never fire you for what happened today. I only came by to talk to you and assure you everything was fine. I knew you'd be too hard on yourself."

"Well, the fact is, I behaved inappropriately and I'm sorry for that."

"Yeah, I got it." It was exactly what he'd hoped to hear her say, but something was still bugging him. "There's one thing I'm concerned about, Kelly."

"What's that?"

"Why the hell do you want to get this Roger clown back?"

"It's something I have to do. And I will," she added with quiet intent. "But honestly, Brandon, please don't give it another thought. I shouldn't have dragged you into my personal issues in the first place."

"Kelly, stop apologizing. I'm the one who insisted that you tell me what was bothering you. If you want to know the truth, I'm glad I'm the one you confided in."

"You are? Why?"

"Because it tells me you trust me, and I appreciate that. You're very important to me."

Her eyes grew soft. "Thank you, Brandon. It means a lot to hear you say that."

"I guess I don't say it often enough." He frowned again. "But that's why it bugs me that you'd want to get this guy back. He hurt you."

"He won't ever hurt me again."

"Good to hear," Brandon said. But he didn't believe it. Kelly was too naïve to know how guys like this Roger creep operated. And Brandon was very much afraid the man knew exactly how to hurt her again. He sipped his wine and considered his next move. "So when does Roger arrive?"

"Not until Monday."

"But he'll still be here for many of the opening week events."

"Yes."

Brandon scowled. Somehow, the thought of watching Kelly coming on to the guy for a whole damn week, pissed him off all over again. To distract himself, he swirled his glass and studied the rich color of the pinot. "Would you like me to talk to him?"

"No!" She bolted straight up. "Thank you for offering, but no. You wouldn't, would you?"

"Yeah," he said matter-of-factly. "If I thought it would help, I would. But it's pretty obvious you'd rather I didn't, so I'll honor your wishes. But I'm warning you, if he makes one wrong move…"

She held up her hand to stop him. "He won't. I won't let him."

"I'm glad." He went back to staring at his wine. "But you're still planning on kissing him?"

Kelly froze. "Um…"

Brandon leaned forward and casually rested his elbows on his knees. "I don't mean to pry, Kelly, but we've got a full agenda for opening week and I'm going to need your undivided attention. So if you're planning on kissing the guy or, you know, getting involved, that could present a problem."

"Brandon, whatever I do with Roger will have no effect whatsoever on my attention to my job."

"I'm not sure I want to take that chance."

She shifted uneasily. "We're just talking about a kiss or two. No big deal."

"It's a big deal if it's done right."

"Oh." She bit her lower lip, considering. "Of course. But Roger won't…well."

He studied her. "Roger won't do it right. Is that what you were going to say?"

"Yes, but what I meant was…" Jittery now, she jumped up from the couch and folded her arms across her chest. "Everything will turn out fine."

"You think?"

She smiled through clenched teeth. "Yes. Absolutely. I know what I'm doing now."

"Oh, I see," he drawled. "Now that I've kissed you, you think you'll be able to show Roger how it's done."

Her jaw tensed up even more as she met his gaze defiantly. "Maybe."

"He won't be here for almost a week," Brandon said. "You sure you'll remember how to do it?"

"Of course," she said, then licked her lips nervously, almost bringing Brandon to his knees. Good thing he was sitting down. And now that he thought about it, why the hell was he sitting here when she was halfway across the room, looking more beautiful than anything he'd seen in a long time, if ever?

Damn, he wanted her. He didn't care if it was stupid. He knew what he wanted. And he always went after what he wanted.

Giving in to the inevitable, he pushed himself up from

the couch and moved toward her. "You weren't thinking of practicing with someone else, were you?"

Her shoulders sagged as if she'd been caught plotting to do just that. "No, of course not."

"Good." Brandon approached slowly, his gaze never leaving hers. "Because I wouldn't want to hear any rumors of unbridled kissing going on."

"You won't, I promise," she murmured as she inched backward.

"I hope not."

"Nothing unbridled, anyway," she said, biting back a smile.

"You think that's funny?" he asked, inches away now. "There's nothing funny about unbridled kissing."

"I'm sure you're right," she said, nodding slowly.

"Oh, believe me, I am." From this close, he could see a dusting of freckles across her cheeks and nose that he'd never noticed before.

"Brandon?" She chewed on her lower lip, nearly driving him crazy. "What are you…"

"Shh," he said, watching her delectable mouth. When it curved into a smile aimed directly at him, he couldn't see any possible way to resist temptation. So he did what any other man would do in his position. He kissed her.

And wondered if he'd ever feasted on anything half as sweet.

Her taste was even more incredible than he remembered and he wanted all of her. He angled his head and deepened the kiss, feeling an urgent need to touch her, to bury himself in her. Enveloping her in his arms, he breathed in her delicious scent as he planted light kisses along her neck, forcing himself to go slowly.

"Brandon, I know you didn't want—"

"Shh." He pushed aside the neckline of her T-shirt and kissed the skin of her shoulder. "I want."

"Are you sure?" she whispered.

"That's my line, sweetheart," he said with a sideways glance.

"Oh." She stared at him, her bright eyes sparkling in the soft light. "Well, I'm sure. I'm really, really sure."

"That's all I wanted to hear."

"Please," she murmured.

"That, too." He slid his hand up her side until he reached the swell of her breast. With his thumb, he did what he'd wanted to do all day, teasing her nipple through the material until he felt it stiffen.

"Please don't stop," she moaned.

"I wouldn't dream of it." He lowered his head and covered her mouth with his. The pleasure was instant, intense. How had he waited all day to do this?

She was eager and opened her mouth to welcome him into her warmth, wrapping her arms around his neck to bring them closer.

"I want my hands on you, Kelly," he muttered.

"Mmm, I want that, too."

It was all the encouragement he needed. He swept her into his arms in an effortless move and walked toward the bed.

"Oh, I like that," she said, her lips curved in a sweet smile.

"Babe, you ain't seen nothing yet."

She cuddled in his arms and rained little kisses along his neck and shoulder. When they reached the bed, he placed her gently on top of the covers, then knelt and straddled her. Reaching for the hem of her T-shirt, he lifted it up and off in one swift move. With her arms raised languidly above her head and her lustrous hair spread over the pillow, she looked like the stuff of Brandon's dreams. He had to force himself to take it slow and easy as he slid his hand under her back and unclipped her bra in one smooth move.

"You are gorgeous," he whispered reverently.

She smiled as she reached up and caressed his cheek, almost as though she couldn't quite believe he was real, either. Brandon wasn't sure he'd ever felt quite so alive as he did in this moment. He bent his head to her breasts and took first one nipple, then the other into his mouth. She gasped and arched off the bed, pushing herself into him, straining his control. Had there ever been a woman so responsive to his touch?

His hands continued to move over her breasts as his mouth carried on his sensual exploration, moving down her taut stomach, stopping here and there to kiss and taste her soft skin. When he reached her heated feminine core, she writhed in anticipation and he rushed to satisfy her and appease his own desperate need as well. He might've lost track of time, aware only of her soft moans of delight and his own heady satisfaction. Through the haze of pleasure, he heard her utter his name.

"Please, Brandon," she said. "I need you, now."

With those words, Brandon moved. He stood and quickly tore off his clothing, tossing his things on the chair nearby. Then he pulled a condom from his pocket and slipped it on. As he made his way back to her, Kelly licked her lips in expectation and Brandon's knees nearly buckled. In that moment, he wanted her more than any woman he'd ever known. The thought meant nothing, he assured himself. It was all the heat of the moment.

Joining her, stretched out beside her, he urged her onto him, gripping her lush bottom with both hands as he guided her sweet center toward his rigid length. As his mouth devoured hers, he plunged himself into her heat and filled her completely.

Their bodies moved in perfect rhythm, as though both had been created for just this moment. The passion was explosive. Brandon had never felt more powerful, more driven by one singular need: her ultimate pleasure.

Her body strained to get closer to his, so close that he could feel her heart pounding against his chest. Her lips found his and molded themselves tenderly to his mouth in a gesture so sweet, it caused a shudder to spread through his body. With a desperation he'd never known, he again thrust himself into her, then again and again. She cried out his name and trembled uncontrollably. He tightened his hold on her, pushing himself to the limit until he answered her with his own deep cry and followed her over the edge.

Four

"So that's what all the fuss is about," Kelly said finally, her soft voice full of wonder.

It had taken a while, but Brandon's head had eventually stopped spinning and his breathing had returned to normal. Now he turned onto his side and, despite being more shaken than he'd like to admit, he flashed a confident smile at her. "Yeah, that's what it's all about. Why do you sound so surprised? I know you've done this before."

"Not like that," she murmured, then quickly looked away and fiddled with the pillow beneath her head.

He reached over and placed his fingers under her chin, urging her to meet his gaze. "Are you telling me your dumb-ass ex-boyfriend never satisfied you?"

She met his gaze warily. "Roger told me I wasn't very good in bed."

Maybe his ears were still ringing from the exertion of a

few minutes ago, because he couldn't have heard her right. So he leaned in close and said, "What did you say?"

"The actual term he used was 'lousy,'" she admitted softly. "According to him, I was *lousy* in bed." She sighed. "When he broke up with me, I made the mistake of asking him why, and that's what he told me."

Brandon wondered if Kelly could see the smoke coming out of his ears because right now he was so angry, he was ready to kill that jackass Roger at the earliest opportunity. This wasn't the time to rant about that, but soon. Very soon. He went up on one elbow and peered at her intently. "He's dead wrong, sweetheart. You know that, right?"

"I do now. Back then, I wasn't so sure."

He shook his head, unwilling to think about that dumb-ass anymore tonight. "Well, that was then and this is now. And I'm sure."

"Really?"

Her smile was tenuous and it almost broke his heart. He touched her soft shoulder with his fingers and said, "Damn it, Kelly, can't you see how tempting you are? Forget what that fool told you. He obviously blamed you for his own inadequacies."

Brandon sat up and leaned against the headboard and pulled her into his arms. "He was wrong, do you hear me? You're amazing. You're hot. I've never . . ." He stopped and took a deep breath. "Let's just say my brains are still bouncing around my head from your hotness."

She smiled brightly and he was suddenly mesmerized all over again by her mouth.

"Okay," she said, nodding slowly. "I believe you."

"Good," he growled. "You should also believe me when I say that guy needs to be taught a serious lesson."

Her smile dimmed. "That's exactly what I plan to do."

She touched his chest and gazed up at him. "Would you do me a favor?"

"Another one?" he said, and chuckled when she smacked his chest lightly. He grabbed her hand before she pulled it back and held it pressed against his skin where it seemed to belong. "Of course I'll do you a favor, sweetheart. What is it?"

"I don't want to hear any words of remorse or blame or embarrassment tomorrow," she said. "Please, Brandon. This was wonderful and I'm so happy. I don't want a shadow to fall on what happened tonight."

He stared at her for a moment, then nodded. "It's a deal. No shadows."

"Thank you." Her smile was sexy as she added, "And by 'thank you,' I mean it in every possible way."

He smoothed a strand of lustrous hair off her cheek. "Now it's your turn to do me a favor. I don't want to hear any more words of thanks. No more undying gratitude from you, do you hear me?"

"But—"

"No." He pressed his finger to her lips. "I didn't do you any favors, believe me. We both made the decision to do what we did, we both had a good time, and that's all there is to it."

She nodded. "You're right. Okay, fine, no more thank yous."

"Thank you." They both laughed and he leaned in to kiss her.

"I really like the way you kiss," Kelly confessed. She moved closer and touched her lips to his and he felt himself spring to life against her.

"In case you couldn't tell, I think it's pretty clear that I really like everything about you." And he proceeded to show her just how much.

* * *

Much later that night, after the second time they'd made love—or was it the third?—Brandon pulled Kelly into his arms and fitted her warm backside against his body.

"Mmm," she said. "That's nice."

"Yeah, it is," he agreed. But part of him questioned what he was doing. Everything felt way too good. That could be a problem. Maybe he should leave now and go to his own room. It had to be after midnight. He could still get a decent night's sleep.

Kelly chose that moment to stretch her muscles, pushing herself even closer against him. On a soft moan, she said, "Oh, I feel so good."

Brandon's head reeled. Was he really thinking of leaving her now? Was he out of his mind?

Not yet. But he would be if he walked out while she was pressed up against him like this.

But if he was going to stay any longer, he knew they needed to talk. So he wrapped his arm around her waist and with his last ounce of brainpower, he murmured, "Hey, you're not falling for me, are you?"

"What?" She managed to twist and roll around until she was facing him and he was glad to see her smiling lightheartedly. "I should ask you the same question."

"Am I falling for you?" he asked, grinning.

She pressed her finger against his chest. "Well, are you?"

He chuckled. "Hey, I know the rules."

"Good," she said in mock seriousness, "because I'm a busy woman and I don't want to have to deal with you mooning all over me in the office."

Smirking, he said, "I'll try to contain myself."

She laughed softly. "I certainly hope so." Her smile

faded as she added, "But since we're talking about it, we should probably decide on a few things."

"Like what?"

"Like the fact that I really don't want the staff discussing our private affair."

"I don't want that, either," he said. "So we'll be discreet."

"Okay, good." Then she grimaced. "Oh dear, what about your family? They'll be here in a few days and I would rather they didn't find out that I'm sleeping with my boss."

Brandon touched her cheek. "I understand." And he did, because even though he had the utmost respect for her, he realized that others might consider their intimate relationship inappropriate.

"So once your family arrives," she said, "we should stop seeing each other."

"Much as I hate to admit it, that's probably a good idea," he said grudgingly, then he ran his hand down her side and stroked her thigh. "But until then…"

Her eyes lit up as she smiled and moved closer. "Mmm, yes. Until then, maybe you could show me again what all the fuss is about."

"Where did you disappear to last night?" Cameron Duke asked when Brandon answered his office phone the next morning. "I tried to call you a few times and finally gave up."

Brandon thought fast for a way to respond to his brother. "I might've been out on a run. What time did you call?"

"First call was around seven, then I tried twice more until about eight."

"Sorry, bro. I guess I plugged my phone in to recharge and forgot all about it. What did you need?"

"Mom was bugging me to call you and confirm the reservations for everything. I finally decided I'd rather talk to Kelly than you, so I gave her a call, but she didn't answer her phone either."

"Huh. Maybe she went into town for dinner."

"Without her phone? Not our Kelly."

"That's weird all right." Brandon rolled his eyes. He hated lying to his brothers but there was no way he could tell them he was sleeping with his assistant. He didn't need the grief they would give him. The fact was, he and Kelly were wrapped up in each other almost from the time they left the office until early this morning. And thinking about it now, he wished he was back in bed with her still, holding her. Inside her. Her soft, naked skin against his.

"So we'll have the use of two golf carts for the wine and vineyard tour?"

"What?" Brandon shook his head to clear his mind of the erotic images he'd conjured up. Damn. "Uh, yeah."

"You okay, bro? Sounds like you've got something else on your mind."

"Yeah, you know how it is. I've got a whole list of stuff." He scratched his jaw, wondering what the hell was going on with his brain. He'd never been distracted by a woman during business hours. Especially when things were so busy. He really needed to shape up and concentrate on the business at hand.

"I definitely know how it is," Cameron said. "I just hope you're ready for the onslaught."

Brandon dragged a hand through his hair and forced himself to swipe another picture of a gorgeous, naked Kelly from his mind. Hell, it wasn't like him to be preoccupied once he was in the office working.

Like his brothers, Brandon left nothing about the business up to chance. He'd held countless management meetings with his hotel and restaurant managers and had brought the entire staff on full-time in the past few weeks before the official opening. Every day, managers would assign different staff members to play guest while those serving meals or cleaning rooms or arranging sightseeing tours or serving wines on the patio could practice their job skills with the same professionalism they would show any true, paying guest. The management team reviewed any problems or difficulties they encountered, then they repeated the process the next day. It was the tried and true way of working out any kinks before they went "live."

The head chef and kitchen staff in the restaurant had worked out the new menu and Brandon knew the reviews would be fantastic. The Mansion on Silverado Trail would soon be the hottest new wine country destination on the map.

His brothers and their wives would arrive on Thursday for a final pre-opening meeting. Then Mom and her friends would arrive Friday morning. Was he ready?

"I'm as ready as I'll ever be," Brandon said, chuckling at the picture of his mom and her girlfriends living it up at the Mansion.

"Glad to hear it," Cameron said, then took a moment to entertain him with the latest stories about baby Jake before they finished the call. As Brandon hung up the phone, he thought about his family and how much they'd all changed over the past year. Who would've guessed how quickly Sally Duke's sons would go from being sworn bachelors to happy family men? Well, two out of three sons, anyway. Cameron and Adam had both succumbed to the charms of two beautiful women, but Brandon wasn't about to follow in their footsteps. No how, no way.

He flashed a determined grin as he vowed, once again, never to fall victim to his mother's matchmaking skills. Sally had denied up and down that she'd had anything to do with Cameron and Adam meeting and falling in love with their respective spouses, but none of the men believed her. Brandon and his brothers still didn't know how she'd managed it, but there was no doubt in their minds that their mother had had something to do with their eventual fall into matrimony.

But not Brandon. It wasn't going to happen to him. Hey, she was welcome to take her best shot. And he had no doubt she would continue to try. Now that he thought about it, he realized he would have to be extra vigilant this weekend.

It wasn't that he didn't love Sally Duke like crazy. On the contrary, he owed her his very life. From the day she'd rescued him from an imminent sentence to juvenile hall, he'd been indebted to her. Brandon had been the worst kind of bad risk, but that hadn't deterred Sally from taking a chance on him.

Sally was a young, wealthy and generous widow whose beloved husband, William, had been a foster kid, too. She'd wanted to give back to the system that had produced such a wonderful guy as William, so she'd adopted three boys all around the same age: Brandon, Adam and Cameron.

Once the three eight-year-olds had learned to trust each other, they'd sworn an oath of allegiance to themselves and Sally. They were blood brothers and nothing would ever split them apart. As part of their pact, they'd vowed never to marry or bring children into this world because they knew that married people hurt each other, and parents— except for Sally—hurt their kids.

Sally had raised them well and they'd grown up to be good, strong, smart men. Well, smart most of the time, Brandon thought. He'd warned his brothers that Sally was out to get them all married, but did they listen? No. Adam met Trish and fell in love. Months later, Cameron reunited with his old flame Julia and discovered he had a son with her, little Jake. Both couples had married recently and were ridiculously happy. Adam and Trish were expecting a little one any day now.

So Adam and Cameron had both fallen flat on the brotherly pledge, but that was okay. Brandon had already explained to them both that he understood they were weak, so he'd sworn to uphold their blood pact all on his own. They'd laughed and given him a hard time. But the fact was, Brandon had been determined long before he met his new brothers, that he would never marry and have kids. Not if it meant carrying on his own son-of-a-bitch father's legacy. And in case he forgot, he just had to recall the hundreds of brutal beatings delivered by his old man after his drug-addicted mother hit the road. He would never forget the lessons those poundings had taught him.

It's not that he begrudged his brothers any happiness. Hell, he was half in love with Trish and Julia himself. But Brandon had seen the worst kind of human behavior and he didn't want his parents' weaknesses rubbing off on any children he might've ever dreamed of having.

For that reason, he kept his relationships with women on a strictly superficial level. He never stayed in a relationship longer than a few weeks, a month or two at the most. Another thing Brandon rarely allowed himself to do was spend the entire night with a woman. He didn't believe in leading them on, giving them hope that an affair with him would be anything more than a momentary fling.

That practice had fallen by the wayside last night with Kelly. He'd planned to leave her room and sleep in his own bed, but he hadn't been able to tear himself away from her sweetness. He'd awakened several times during the night with an urgent need to be inside her. And this morning, they'd showered together and made love again.

The thought of Kelly and the way she'd looked, with her

body glistening in the soap-scented water, almost made him groan out loud.

It stunned him to think that he'd actually had sex with Kelly. She was a fascinating woman and he'd known that for years, but now he'd seen a completely different side of her. And he wanted more. She'd been so uninhibited and sweet, so unlike any other woman he'd been involved with in the past.

It was a good thing they'd reaffirmed their ground rules last night. The absolute last thing he wanted was to hurt Kelly, so he was glad they'd talked things over. It was good to see her smile as she reassured him that it wouldn't be a problem for her if they kept seeing each other. She insisted they were just having a good time and she was happy to be learning so much about the art of seduction. But, she'd said, there was no way in the world she would ever be dumb enough to fall in love with him.

His mind deep in thought, he didn't notice when Kelly walked into his office until she placed a hot cup of coffee on his desk blotter.

Looking up at her, he murmured "Hey there, stranger," and was about to grab her hand and pull her into his lap when she cut him off brusquely with a sharp look of warning.

"Good morning, Brandon." She said it loudly and followed it with an overly obvious nudge of her chin, just as their concierge manager rushed in behind her. "Serge has a matter of some urgency he'd like to discuss with you."

Serge paced in front of his desk. "Do you have a **moment**, Brandon? A problem has arisen with the new tour company."

"Sure." He gave Kelly a brief but meaningful nod, then turned to Serge. "What can I do for you?"

* * *

Kelly poured water into the coffeepot and stifled a yawn. It was no wonder she was tired. Besides attending to all the general preparations and last-minute emergencies that went with the grand opening of the hotel, she'd also spent the entire night making love with Brandon. That meant she had gotten almost no sleep and now her body ached in all sorts of places she never even knew she had. Not that she was complaining. No way. And she refused to feel guilty. In fact, she felt wonderful.

She still couldn't quite believe that Brandon had simply appeared at her hotel room door. She was even more incredulous over the fact that she'd spent hours after that having spectacular sex with him. It was so much more fun when you did it right, she thought.

But then this morning as she got dressed, she began to worry about how Brandon would react to seeing her in the office. Even though they'd made a pact that neither of them would feel remorseful or embarrassed, she couldn't be sure. Maybe she'd made a huge mistake by sleeping with him.

Or maybe not. After all, it was sex, nothing more. There were no emotions involved. She was just having a little affair with a man millions of other women would kill for. No pressure.

By the time she walked into the office, she'd worked herself into a state of anxiety, wondering over and over again what in the world she'd been thinking the night before. Had she lost her mind? Why had she slept with him?

But then she'd walked into Brandon's office and he'd smiled broadly and reached for her. And she knew why.

It had been wonderful and totally worth it.

She should've known Brandon would do it right. Besides

being tall, gorgeous, utterly captivating and totally sexy, he'd lived a charmed life ever since he'd been adopted by Sally Duke at the age of eight.

Sally had once given Kelly a thumbnail sketch of Brandon's life, starting with him being a high school honors student and an All-American football player in college. He was drafted into the NFL where he played quarterback for many years before becoming a sports commentator for the premier sports news station in the country. But he'd grown weary of the limelight and had joined his brothers' hotel and real estate development team a few years ago.

Sally had also confided that the man attracted women like flies. Kelly was already well aware of that. For the past four years, she'd been charged with the job of keeper of the keys to the inner sanctum. In other words, she screened every woman who called or came by to speak with Brandon. Depending on his instructions, she would either put them through or put them off.

Never in her wildest dreams did she think she would end up as one of those women. The thought didn't appeal to her as she sat down at her desk and powered up her computer.

"I'm not one of those women," she argued with herself, recalling their conversation late last night. "We've got an arrangement. This is a temporary situation only."

But now she could see why all those women had had such stars in their eyes. Brandon's touch had put a twinkle in her eye, too. The thought made her smile as she gathered the mail and began to open each envelope, sorting the enclosed documents and letters into several different piles, depending on priority. When she caught herself humming off key, she giggled. Then she froze.

"What in the world was that?"

Kelly never giggled. What was wrong with her? Was she coming down with something? She held her hand against her forehead to check her temperature, but her skin was perfectly cool and dry. She was pretty sure there was only one answer to the question. She was…happy?

Okay, happy was a good word to describe how she felt. She couldn't believe her good luck and even though Brandon had warned her not to say the words out loud, she couldn't help but be grateful. She wished she could thank him for his…what? His *assistance?* No, that made it sound like he was helping her bake a cake. Grateful for his *special friendship?* Kelly shivered. No, that sounded vaguely icky.

"For his expertise," she said aloud, and nodded at the description. "I'm in training." She smiled again. It sounded much better, more subtle, than the other choices. After all, she often went for training on new computer systems and software programs, so why not sexual expertise? It made perfect sense and besides, it was true. She really was in training to improve her sexual proficiency. She was the student and Brandon was the master.

She could only imagine the syllabus.

She giggled again. Okay, maybe she was getting a little carried away.

"Kelly, do you have the Redmond file?"

"It's right here, Brandon." She managed to refrain from calling him *Obi-Wan,* then stifled another giggle.

"What's the smile for?" Brandon asked genially.

"I'm just in a good mood," she said. "Coffee'll be ready in a few minutes."

"Thanks," he said, and strolled into his office, closing the door behind him.

She knew Brandon had a conference call starting momentarily that would last an hour or more. She planned to use that time to check on Roger's conference agenda. He and the employees of his small, high-powered hedge-fund company would arrive on Monday. They had reserved two mid-sized conference rooms each day as well as one of the small banquet rooms each evening for dinners and a special event or two. But Kelly remembered that the schedule showed that Thursday night was a free night, during which the attendees could dine at their choice of any one of Napa's world-class restaurants or go off to sample wines at any number of local wineries.

Kelly planned to lure Roger to her room Thursday night, get him all hot and bothered, then kick him out. That would teach him a thing or two. And Kelly looked forward to being the one to teach him. In fact, she was eager for the chance to show her ex-boyfriend a few of the incredible moves Brandon had showed her. She already felt more sure of herself and more sure of her sensuality and attractiveness, thanks to Brandon. Ever since yesterday morning when he got all tongue-tied while gawking at her and her new look, she'd felt her confidence soar. She really appreciated that his gawking turned out to be good in all the right ways.

The telephone rang, startling her. She grabbed the receiver quickly so the ringing wouldn't disturb Brandon's conference call. "Mr. Duke's office, Kelly Meredith speaking."

"It's Bianca Stephens," a breathless voice said. "Let me speak with Brandon immediately."

"I'm sorry, Ms. Stephens, Brandon is on a conference call and can't be disturbed."

The woman gasped. "What? Well, interrupt him. Tell him I'm waiting. I know he'll want to talk to me."

"I'm sure you're right," Kelly said, trying not to roll her eyes, "but he's on a long-distance call with several business clients and his partners. I'll have to take a message and have him get back to you."

"Kathy, do you know who I am?"

"Yes, I do, Ms. Stephens, and it's Kelly."

"Whatever," she said. "Look, just slip a note under his nose. I know he'll take my call."

"Except he gave me instructions not to interrupt him, and since he signs my paycheck, I generally do as he asks. I'm terribly sorry, but I will give him your message."

"What did you say your name was?"

"Kelly," she said distinctly. "Kelly Meredith."

"Well, Kelly," Bianca said with a tone that implied that she was talking down to a particularly stupid first grader. "I'll be sure to tell Brandon how uncooperative you have been."

"Yes, ma'am. And I'll be sure to give him your message."

"You'd better," she said imperiously. "He won't be happy to find out he missed my call."

"I'm sure that's true," Kelly said. "I—"

But the line was already dead.

Shaken, Kelly stared at the phone. "Gosh, I hope I don't forget to give him that message."

After hanging up the phone, she had to get up and walk around the office. She stretched her arms and rolled her neck around, just to get rid of some of the anger she was feeling. Of course she knew who Bianca Stephens was. She was the daughter of a former secretary of defense who hosted a national morning talk show. She was model-thin and Playmate gorgeous, and she was probably really smart, too. Damn her.

Walking into the kitchenette to pour a soda, Kelly gave herself a stern lecture. She understood that there had always been women like Bianca Stephens in Brandon's life and there always would be. They were supermodels, heiresses, actresses and designers. Some were nice and some were awful, like Bianca Stephens. It didn't matter to Brandon. He dated them because they looked good on his arm and probably in his bed, although she didn't want to dwell too closely on that possibility. The plain fact was that Kelly was disappointed by the fact that Brandon would ever want to be with anyone as rude as Bianca Stephens.

Kelly took a moment to thank her lucky stars that she wasn't so emotionally involved with Brandon that she cared one way or the other, but she had to admit it was upsetting to be treated as though she were nothing but the hired help.

That thought stopped Kelly in her tracks. She took a few deep breaths, shook her hair back, did some more shoulder rolls, then headed for her desk feeling cranky and restless.

"Not to put too fine a point on it," she muttered as she sat in her chair. "But *hired help* is exactly what you are."

Fine. Didn't mean she had to dwell on it. She grabbed her knifelike letter opener and pulled out another short stack of mail. Being the hired help wasn't the issue, she insisted to herself. It was having to deal with rude people like Bianca who looked down her nose at someone like Kelly just because she was hired to answer the phone. The fact was, Bianca thought she was better than everyone else, not just Kelly.

But that wasn't the real problem, Kelly realized as she slashed open another letter. She'd fielded these sorts of phone calls from petulant women in the past and she'd always let them roll off her back. So what was different about Bianca's call?

"You wouldn't care so much if you hadn't slept with him," she whispered aloud as she tossed several letters into a file for Brandon's review. With a frown, she ripped open a small parcel and tried to deny the words.

Was that why she was so upset? Did she suddenly care too much for Brandon? She didn't think so. She *cared* for him, of course, but she certainly didn't, well, *love* him, God forbid. There was no way she would ever let that happen. Not only had they talked about it and she'd assured him that she'd never fall for him, but also, she knew better!

But, thinking about it now, she was willing to admit to feeling a little sensitive. After all, they had spent last night doing the most intimate things a man and a woman could do together. So of course she was a bit distressed. Who wouldn't be? But she'd snap out of it, quick. Because if she didn't, she'd wind up with black and blue marks from kicking herself in the behind. No way would she ever allow herself to be that much of a twit.

The telephone rang and she jumped. "Now what?"

Hoping it wasn't Bianca calling back, she grabbed it and answered in her most officious voice.

"Hello, Kelly dear. It's Sally Duke."

"Oh, Mrs. Duke, hello," Kelly said, and relaxed. Brandon's mother was always so lovely and kind. "How are you?"

"Fine, sweetie. I'm looking forward to seeing you this weekend."

"I'm looking forward to seeing you, too." She opened one of the folders on her desk. "I've got your itinerary right here and I see you'll be arriving around two o'clock Friday afternoon. The limousine will be waiting for you at the airport. Did Brandon make dinner reservations for you?"

"I hope so. Would you mind checking for me?"

"Not at all. I don't see anything noted in the file, but I'll ask Brandon as soon as he's off his conference call. We'll make sure you're taken care of."

"I know you will and I must admit I'm excited," Sally

said. "There are hundreds of fabulous restaurants in Napa I'd love to try."

"Oh, me, too."

Sally paused, then said, "Kelly, dear, is something wrong? You don't sound like yourself."

It was not a good thing when the boss's mother could tell you were in a blue mood.

"No, I'm fine," Kelly insisted. "Or I will be. I just had to deal with something unpleasant."

"Something or someone?"

Kelly sighed, knowing she'd already said too much. "Really, it's nothing I can't handle."

"Ah," Sally said. "Some*one*."

Kelly laughed ruefully. "You're good at that."

"I raised three boys. I've learned to read nuance."

Kelly laughed again as her mind raced to change the subject. It wouldn't do to involve Mrs. Duke in her problems. "I see Brandon's taking you and your friends on a private tour of the winery on Saturday. That'll be fun."

"Oh, we'll have a ball," Sally said jovially. "Now Kelly, we're having a family dinner Saturday night at the hotel restaurant. Adam and Cameron and their wives will be there and it would be wonderful if you could join us. That is, if you're free. You always do so much for all of us. We feel like you're a member of the family."

Sudden tears sprang to her eyes and Kelly quickly brushed them away. Her own mother had died when she was twelve and she still missed her every day. Her father was very much alive, but he lived back in Vermont near her two sisters and their families. She missed them, too, but she could always pick up the phone and say hello. She couldn't do that with her mom.

"As far as I know, I'm free," she said. "And I would love to join you, Mrs. Duke. Thank you so much for asking me." She had the sudden thought that Brandon might bring a date to the dinner, but told herself it didn't matter. The invitation had come from his mother.

"Wonderful," Sally exclaimed. "Oh, by the way, how was your trip to the spa? Did they do everything they promised?"

"It was amazing," Kelly said. "Thank you so much for recommending it."

"I had a fabulous time when I was there last year," Sally said. "So when you mentioned you wanted a bit of a makeover, I thought it would be the perfect place for you."

"It was."

"I'm so glad. I can't wait to see all the fun changes in you."

They hung up from the call, and Kelly spent the rest of the morning answering emails and scheduling conference calls for future projects. She almost wished she wasn't so organized because she could've used a few more hours concentrating on something other than her thoughts. Anything would be preferable to being completely distracted by memories of Brandon and everything they'd done together the night before and early this morning. It was impossible to think straight when she remembered the way he'd touched her, the way his body had quickened inside her, the way his breath had lingered hot on her skin. She thought of the words he'd used, the pleasure he'd shown her, the urgency of their needs, and almost moaned out loud.

"Oh, God." She gulped in air and grabbed her soda to soothe her parched throat. She needed to concentrate on her job, but it wasn't working. She continued to daydream about the way he made her feel, the places he'd touched her, the words he'd whispered in her ear, the heights he'd driven her to.

She stared at the red light on the phone. Thank goodness
Brandon was still on the conference call because if he were
to walk out and take one look at her, he would know what
she'd been thinking. And if he knew she was obsessing
over their lovemaking, he would probably accuse her of
falling for him. But nothing could be further from the
truth. There was no way she would ever fall for Brandon
Duke. She'd never been that big of a fool.

Forcing herself to concentrate on work, she got a lot
done in the next hour. Still, every few minutes or so, she
caught herself imagining his arms around her. The man
had a gift, that was for sure.

She spent part of her lunch hour at her desk, eating a
sandwich and paying some bills. Brandon left for a meeting
outside of the office, so after lunch, Kelly placed all his
messages—including Bianca's—on his desk and took the
opportunity to go for a short walk along the brick path that
skirted the vineyards. It was a beautiful fall day and the
leaves on the vines were every shade of orange, red and
burnt sienna. She waved to a few of the winery staff who
stood a few rows away, testing the vines for ripeness.

She glanced up at the six floors of terraced balcony
suites that graced the hillside, with their French doors
and elegant patio furniture, then looked over at the many
sophisticated, private two-bedroom *maisons* that swept
across the length of the hill. She couldn't help but feel
a glow of pride whenever she thought of the small but
important role she'd played in the development of the
luxurious Mansion at Silverado Trail.

With its ivy-covered stucco walls and Mediterranean
style, the resort was a first-class mix of old-world charm
and modern elegance. The restaurant had already earned
a rare three stars from an international travel guide. No

wonder she was so justifiably proud of the company she worked for.

In three days, the first guests would arrive, anxious to take part in the grand opening weekend that included full participation in the grape harvest and autumn festival that followed. There would be lovely dinners and wine tastings and a gala celebration Saturday night.

Kelly had worked on the opening events for months. She considered the project her baby. She had sweated out every last detail, down to the color of the ribbon for the cutting ceremony in the lobby that would take place Friday afternoon when the first guests checked in.

But since the project had started, several major changes had occurred in her life. She needed to be at the top of her game in order to focus her energies on the week ahead. First, she hadn't counted on ever having to see Roger again. Now, within days, he would be here and her plan would swing into action.

But a more important change was her involvement with Brandon. Never in her wildest dreams had she imagined she'd be caught up in a lovely affair with Brandon Duke. It was a major distraction and she knew she would require every last ounce of brainpower, discretion and good judgment in her arsenal to make it through the week working so closely with him. Not only that, but she would have to be especially careful that the hotel staff and Brandon's family never suspected a thing.

She was certain it wouldn't be a problem. They'd already decided to end their affair once Brandon's family arrived. And, then she'd have Roger to deal with.

But for the moment, she just breathed in the crisp air and looked around at the welcome signs of autumn. Growing up in Vermont, she'd always been able to recognize the telltale signs of each new season. But here in California, where the hillsides seemed a permanent shade of green and the weather was distressingly mild even in winter, the hints were much more subtle: the dappled hue of the falling leaves, a trace of mesquite in the air, the delicate play of shadows and light on the mountains at sunset.

She loved it here in Napa, but she had to admit she'd be happy to return home to Dunsmuir Bay in a few weeks. She had a charming duplex apartment with a view of the bay and a number of good friends she would be glad to see again. And of course she loved her job and her spacious office at Duke headquarters.

Once she was home, she would be long finished with the Roger Project. She planned to start dating again as soon as possible and would have no reason to ever sleep with Brandon again. Especially since she had no intention of jeopardizing her position at Duke Development, it was absolutely imperative that she go back to being the practical, professional, well-organized assistant Brandon deserved.

And that meant no more sex with Brandon, ever again.

She would use those words as a mantra because within a few days, they would become reality. *No more sex with Brandon,* she repeated and emphasized the words with a firm nod of her head as she turned and walked back to the office.

Five

The lunch meeting took longer than Brandon had expected and now he wasn't looking forward to playing catch-up. He stalked down the hall toward his suite of offices and braced himself for the onslaught of urgent messages he knew Kelly would hand him as soon as he walked in. He had half a mind to toss every last message in the trash, grab Kelly and go for a drive into the hills where they could hide out for the rest of the day.

He chuckled, figuring he was lucky he still had that half of his mind left, considering the things he and Kelly had done the night before. An erotic image of her gorgeous, naked body spread across the bed flashed in his mind and he gritted his teeth to keep from embarrassing himself in the middle of the hotel. Damn. If that wasn't enough to make him crazed, the fact that he planned to stay with her again tonight was almost enough to drive him the rest of the way to madness. But what a way to go.

Back in his office, he sorted through his message slips, crumpling one from Bianca, a woman he dated once in a while, and tossing it into the trash can. One thing he didn't need right now was another distraction.

He forced himself to concentrate on work, but stimulating thoughts of Kelly kept circling his mind whenever his vigilance slipped. He needed to keep his mind on business. And there was plenty of business to think about.

His brothers would arrive Thursday, two days from now, and things would really start cooking. No doubt, there would be several last-minute meetings, emergency conference calls, inspections and tests of various departments before the festivities began Friday. His mother and her friends would be arriving then, along with the first official guests of the Mansion.

The guest list included numerous wealthy wine lovers, a reviewer from a prestigious travel magazine, several old friends of the Duke brothers and a well-heeled state official they'd done business with. And, lest he forgot, Kelly's idiot ex-boyfriend. Roger and company wouldn't arrive until Monday, but that was still too soon as far as he was concerned.

Part of him still couldn't believe he'd succumbed to Kelly's pleas for help in luring the jerk back. Not that he minded helping her, he thought, his blood pumping faster as he once again pictured her beneath him. No, he didn't mind that at all. But if she truly had the intention of taking Roger to bed, Brandon wouldn't hesitate to obstruct her at every turn.

Hell. Brandon knew if he was smart, he would cancel his plans for Kelly tonight and call last night's passionate activities a one-time-only deal. He knew they were playing with fire and shouldn't continue sleeping with each other.

And he knew he should be the one to call it quits, right now, before they got involved any further. Kelly would understand. They'd already had that discussion.

But every time he thought about cutting her loose, he changed his mind. He couldn't bring himself to do it. He just wanted her too damn much. He also knew those feelings would subside. They always did. He made sure of it. And when that happened, Kelly and he would go back to being companionable working partners and bring the sexual side of their relationship to a civil, friendly end. No mess, no fuss.

Their affair was a strictly temporary arrangement and they were both consenting adults. Once this whole ugly Roger situation passed, Brandon and Kelly would settle down and get back to work and everything would be fine. Fine as wine. No problem.

The following evening, Brandon coaxed Kelly to come to dinner with him at a charming trattoria in downtown Napa. They dressed casually, both glad to escape from the hotel for a few hours. They spent the meal having a good time, chatting about business and family matters. Kelly told Brandon about her sisters and their families and Brandon mentioned his mother's new project to track down her deceased husband's brother.

"Sally's husband, William Duke, had a brother, Tom," Brandon explained as they shared an antipasto platter. "When their parents died, the boys were sent to an orphanage in San Francisco."

Kelly nodded as she filled her small plate with a delicious mixture of baby artichokes, roasted peppers and grilled zucchini. "Sally told me her husband was the reason she wanted to adopt you three boys."

"That's right. Bill's dream was to symbolically give

back to other kids he'd met in the system by adopting children of his own, but he passed away before he could do it."

"It was good of Sally to carry out his dream."

Brandon grinned as he sipped his wine. "I thank my lucky stars every day that she did."

"Has she had any luck finding Bill's brother?"

"Not yet. Apparently the orphanage was a pretty grim place and the boys ran away a few times. Bill told Sally that he was finally adopted, but his brother was still stuck there. Years later, when he was old enough to conduct a search, he found that the orphanage had burned to the ground and all the records were destroyed."

"Oh, that's terrible. Does Sally know if Bill's brother survived?"

"Yeah, Tom would've turned eighteen by the time the fire happened, so he'd be out on his own. But Bill tried to track him down and couldn't find him. His best hope was that Tom was adopted and his adoptive parents changed his name."

"I hope so," Kelly said. "That place sounds awful."

"Yeah. Anyway, Sally's got her work cut out for her."

Kelly reached for an olive. "Please tell her I'll be glad to help if she needs someone to do research. You know I love a challenge."

He smiled at her. "Thanks, Kelly, I appreciate that. I'll let her know."

"That was fun," Kelly said as they strolled back to her hotel room. "And the pasta was delicious. I'm so full."

"Yeah, me too," Brandon said. "I'm glad we could get away for a while. We won't have much of a chance to leave from here on out."

"I know." Kelly stared up at the cloudless night sky.

Countless stars stretched from one horizon to the other and the full moon lit the way along the terrace path.

"It's a beautiful evening," she said.

"Still warm out," Brandon remarked. "It's a perfect night for a swim."

She raised her eyebrows. "I'm not sure it's that warm."

"It is for what I have in mind," he said, grabbing hold of her hand. "Come with me."

Puzzled but willing, Kelly allowed him to change direction and he led her to the owner's *maison* where he was staying. The sleekly comfortable bungalow had been built into the hillside beyond the main building. It was large, with two bedrooms and a vaulted ceiling and a fireplace in the living room. Shuttered French doors opened on to a cozy patio.

Brandon led her through the doors to a lovely space surrounded by a wall of shrubs and flowers and weeping olive trees. A rustic flagstone patio encircled a small hot tub built for two.

Kelly glanced around, intrigued. The thick, lush vegetation grew high around the patio and assured her that they had complete privacy out here.

"It's beautiful," she said, gazing at Brandon.

"I think so." He pressed a button on the wall by the doorway and Kelly watched, smiling, as bubbles began to rise in the water.

Then Brandon reached for Kelly's jacket, slipped it off, folded it and laid it on the chaise. Kelly did the same for him, and together they made quick work of removing their clothes before stepping into the warm bubbling water.

"Oh, it's heaven," she said, and slid down until the water covered her shoulders.

Brandon followed her into the spa and sat on the step, then pulled her onto his lap, facing him.

"Yes, this is definitely heaven." Touching her cheeks with both hands, he leaned forward and kissed her. As his lips touched hers, Kelly's mind emptied of all thought and everything within her focused on this one man and his thrilling touch.

He took his time with her, working his magic, kissing her, touching her, his tongue gently stroking hers. She floated on a sea of pleasure, weightless in his arms.

He cupped her breasts in his hands and bent his head to taste one, then the other. "You're so beautiful."

"Brandon," she whispered.

"I want to make love with you."

"Yes," she said.

He stood up in the water with her in his arms and she wrapped her legs around his waist. He eased her down onto his length and she drew him in so deeply, so fully, she wondered if she would ever feel this complete again. Then he grabbed hold of her bottom and squeezed gently, causing a jolt of rapture to rush through her. She cried out her pleasure as he moved inside her, stroking her faster and harder, plunging deeper, then deeper still. She moved with him as pure sensation pulsated and radiated from her center outward, stirring every part of her body and soul.

She ran her hands over the taut, rippling muscles of his back, relishing his strength as his powerful hips thrust into her, urging her toward completion. She felt her body melt into his and with a guttural groan of release, he let himself join her, flying headlong into an abyss of pure ecstasy.

The next day, Kelly finally began to see that there were flaws in her Roger Plan. As the days had passed and the weekend loomed, her original plot to seek revenge against Roger was becoming less and less important to her. That was fine, of course; she really needed to get over Roger once and for all.

But now she couldn't quite recall the hurt and emptiness anymore. The truth was, in the last few days, whenever she searched her mind, heart and soul for traces of the sadness she'd felt since Roger broke up with her, she couldn't find any painful remnants. That was truly amazing, and she knew she had Brandon to thank for her new acceptance. He'd helped her see that Roger had been wrong; she was perfectly capable of attracting a man. She wasn't lousy in bed. On the contrary, she thought with a happy smile, she was pretty darn good in bed. And she was a good kisser, too. Brandon didn't seem to have any complaints, and he would know, wouldn't he?

But now, since Brandon was in her bed every night, he was also beginning to show up in her daydreams during office hours. If she wasn't ruthlessly diligent, she would find herself sighing like a teenager whenever he walked by her desk.

She'd managed to cover up her reaction the few times it had happened, going so far as to fake a coughing fit one time, then making a quick reference to a missing invoice another time. She needed to get a grip. Not just for Brandon, but for herself.

For goodness sake, where was that practical-minded girl who wouldn't be caught dead giggling or mooning over anyone, *especially* her boss? The last thing she wanted was for him to see her pining over him!

She would drive herself crazy if she didn't nip these feelings in the bud right now. They had ground rules, had she forgotten? She was absolutely forbidden to fall for Brandon Duke. Not only would it never work out, but she'd wind up losing the job she loved.

Any time she caught herself wondering, hoping, or

wishing that she and Brandon could be together for real, all she had to do was log on to his personal address list and count the number of women he'd so nicely dumped over the past year or two, with nothing but a lovely parting gift to remember him by. Kelly should know; she'd been the one to purchase and send out most of those lovely gifts on his behalf.

It didn't help her cause that Brandon had come to her room every night this week and stayed until morning. He would always leave well before Housekeeping came on duty, knowing it wouldn't be appropriate for the rest of the staff to know they were sleeping together. He was an amazing lover, and every night they laughed and talked and…played. And recently, during the day, he had taken to piercing her with long, intense looks that could easily drive her to sin.

What was a girl to do?

She gave herself a mental shake and told herself to get back to work. There was plenty to get done today and it was about time she concentrated on earning her paycheck.

"It is dreck!" head chef Jean Pierre exclaimed, his lips curved in revulsion.

"Are you insane? It's the finest Montepulciano produced in Tuscany in fifty years," Antonio Stellini, the wine steward, countered.

"Italian," Jean Pierre muttered in disdain. "It figures, no?"

"What's that supposed to mean, you French fruitcake?"

Jean Pierre turned on Brandon. "*Qu'est-ce que c'est* fruitcake?"

It was Thursday morning and Brandon had spent the last hour running interference between his autocratic head chef, Jean Pierre, and Antonio, the brilliant sommelier he'd recently hired. The two were in a power struggle over the choice of wine pairings for Saturday night's special tasting menu. Brandon walked out of the meeting feeling a special kinship to King Solomon for effectively negotiating a reasonable solution to an impossible problem. Of course, they'd now added three new premium wines to the elaborate menu, that would have to be reprinted immediately.

Later that afternoon, Cameron and Adam and their wives arrived. Brandon had arranged for each couple to stay in their own private *maison* complete with fireplace, private spa patio and stunning views of the valley. Trish and Julia were able to indulge in soothing massages and facials while he and his brothers held meetings with their key managers.

That night, Brandon hosted dinner for his brothers and their wives in the hotel dining room. He'd tried to convince Kelly to join them, but she'd demurred, saying she had some personal matters to attend to. He couldn't tell if she was telling the truth, but he'd finally let it go. Then, throughout the superb meal, he struggled to avoid thinking about her and the fact that he missed her.

As the main dishes were cleared away and dessert orders were taken, Adam's wife, Trish, turned to Brandon. "I wish Kelly could've joined us. You're not making her work late, are you?"

"No way," Brandon said. "I invited her, but she said she had some personal stuff to take care of."

Cameron shrugged. "Can't blame her. After all, who really wants to have dinner with their boss?"

Brandon said nothing as he made a point of keeping a vigilant watch on the wait staff.

"She looks wonderful," Julia said after finishing the last sip of her wine. "What did she do to herself?"

Baffled, Brandon shook his head. "Some kind of makeover. Not sure why. Who can figure these things out?"

Trish laughed. "Women love to get themselves made over. It's fun."

Brandon shot her a skeptical look. "If you say so. I've got to tell you, though. I love women, but I'll never understand what makes them tick."

Adam chuckled. "Whereas, we men are an open book."

"Exactly," Brandon said, jabbing the air with his finger. "No games. No subterfuge. No *makeovers*." He used air quotes to emphasize the last word.

With a laugh, Julia turned to Trish. "Kelly went to Orchids, didn't she?"

"That's right," Trish said. "It's supposed to be fabulous. Didn't Sally go there last year? I think I remember her raving about the seaweed massage one day when we were sitting around her pool."

"Wait, Mom went to a spa?" Brandon asked, incredulous.

"Yes," Trish said easily. "Just last summer, with Bea and Marjorie."

Brandon felt a chill cross his shoulders. "To the same place Kelly went to?"

"I think so. You should ask her."

Brandon watched as Adam's wife rubbed her ever-expanding stomach. He thought of the eight-month-old baby waiting inside there, all set to emerge and be spoiled silly by its aunts and uncles and one doting grandmother.

"God," Trish said, "I would love to spend an entire weekend getting pampered and rubbed and polished and primped."

"Sounds like heaven," Julia agreed with a happy sigh.

Brandon had worked in hotels and resorts long enough to recognize the allure of an elegant spa for female guests.

And hell, after having spent ten years in the NFL, he could readily admit to the restorative benefits of being pummeled by a physical therapist. He even enjoyed relaxing in a hot tub once in a while. But that had little to do with therapy, he thought, as the vivid memory of a naked Kelly in his own spa almost made him double over.

He gritted his teeth and continued to listen to his sisters-in-law wax poetic over this fabulous spa his mother had recommended to Kelly. They made it sound like some magical realm where dreams came true. His eyes narrowed. "What was the big deal about that place?"

"Oh, there's every type of wonderful massage, of course," Julia said. "You feature several of them here, along with your mud baths and yoga classes. But this place Sally found is designed for women only, and even though they offer more rigorous activities like hiking and horseback riding, they also concentrate on every aspect of a woman's body and mind. You're pampered from the minute you walk into the lobby. But that's not the best part."

Brandon exchanged glances with his brothers, who both looked clueless. "Go on."

"It offers total makeovers," Trish explained. "They do hairstyling and give makeup tips and even offer clothing advice, with suggestions for colors and shapes that will better suit one's body type and season palette."

"Season palette?" Brandon said. It was like they were speaking in a foreign language.

"Oh, and don't forget the meals," Julia added. "They serve these artfully designed portions that look beautiful on the plate but contain maybe fifty calories total."

"That's why I wouldn't last more than one weekend," Trish said, laughing.

"You and me both," Julia said.

Brandon had heard enough. Why hadn't he known that his own mother had been giving Kelly advice on this makeover nonsense? Of course, now that he was aware of the reality of the situation, he had to admit he shouldn't have been completely surprised that his mother had taken Kelly on as her latest matchmaking project.

Didn't it just figure? Sally had made no secret of the fact that she wanted all three of her sons married with children, and she'd accomplished two-thirds of her goal. Now there was just Brandon left to fall.

He knew his mother, knew how sneaky she could be, so he'd been hypervigilant for months now. But Kelly had no idea about Sally's nefarious plotting and had innocently played along with her to such an extent that she'd actually taken two weeks of vacation to the very place his mother had recommended.

Kelly had returned from her holiday a completely new woman. And, lo and behold, her return to the office had signaled the beginning of an affair that he—against his better judgment—didn't want to end.

Brandon scowled. If his mother thought Kelly could lure him to the altar with a change of hairstyle and a few wardrobe modifications, she was sadly mistaken.

And how much did Kelly really know about his mother's desire to marry him off? Frankly, he hesitated to lay any blame at Kelly's feet. This situation had Sally's fingerprints all over it. And, yes, Kelly had told him that the makeover was all about getting Roger back. But had she been telling him the truth?

"I don't like that look at all," Adam said, studying him carefully.

Brandon picked up his wineglass and swirled it thoughtfully. "Tough."

"What's going on in that bizarre head of yours?"

Cameron said. "You look like you're about ready to chew on some nails."

"I'm about ready to chew on something," he muttered.

There was a knock on her door and Kelly's stomach tingled. She couldn't help it. She'd spent a quiet evening catching up on reading and watching television, secure in the knowledge that now that his family was on the scene, Brandon would no longer be spending his nights with her. She'd accepted it and insisted to herself that the only emotion she felt was gratitude. She would be grateful for the rest of her life for the past few wonderful nights with Brandon.

But now he was here and she was bubbling with happiness. That was absurd. Okay, yes, she liked him and all, but she really needed to calm down. It wouldn't do to behave like a giddy schoolgirl every time she saw him. Besides, he probably just wanted to assure her once and for all that they would no longer be spending their nights together. She was okay with that.

She took a few quick, deep breaths and forced herself to walk calmly to the door instead of racing like the wind to greet him.

"Brandon," she said. "I didn't think I'd see you tonight."

"I need to ask you something," he said as he walked in, immediately filling the room with his masculine presence and his faint but intoxicating scent of leather and spice.

"Of course, anything," she said. "Did you enjoy your dinner?"

"What? Oh, yeah. Dinner was fantastic. Jean Pierre outdid himself."

"I'm so glad. It was nice to see Trish and Julia again. They both look so beautiful, and your brothers look so happy."

"Yeah. Nice. Beautiful. Happy."

"Is something wrong?"

He stared at her and frowned. "You're beautiful, too."

"Thank you, I think."

"No, you are," he assured her, studying her features. "You always were, but I guess I didn't realize it before. But you are beautiful, Kelly."

"Brandon, what's wrong? What happened tonight?"

"Nothing." He paced a few steps, then returned to stand directly in front of her. "Let me ask you something. Did my mother suggest that you get a makeover?"

"Your mother? Heavens, no."

"She didn't give you the idea?"

"No." It was Kelly's turn to frown. "Why?"

"Didn't you go to the same place where she went a year or so ago?"

"Well, yes, I did." She led him over to the kitchen area and grabbed her water glass. After taking a long sip, she said, "Your mother only recommended Orchids after I told her I was interested in finding a spa where I could…" She stopped and glanced up at Brandon's expression. "Brandon, what's this all about?"

He stared at her for a moment before looking away. He stalked slowly in one direction, then another, like a caged animal, then stopped and met her gaze again. "You're sure my mother didn't suggest that you needed to get a makeover?"

Kelly blinked. "My goodness, Brandon. Your mother is the sweetest woman in the world. She would never say anything like that to me."

"You're sure?"

"Of course I'm sure. She simply recommended a place after I asked her for suggestions."

His eyes continued to focus on her, then he nodded briefly. "Okay, good."

"I'm surprised you would think so poorly of your mother."

"Whoa." He held up his hand to stop her. "Believe me, I love my mother and don't think poorly of her at all. It's just that she's been known to manipulate a situation or two, and I was just concerned that she might've given you some unsolicited advice."

"Well, please don't be concerned on my account. I simply mentioned my interest in, you know, making a few changes to my hair and...well, other things, and your mother gave me the name of the spa she'd visited. I took it from there."

He seemed satisfied with her explanation. "Okay, I'm glad to hear it."

She shook her head, realizing he was in a mood and she wouldn't get much more of an explanation from him. "Would you like a glass of wine or something?"

"Yeah, something. Come here." With that, he reached out to her with both hands, pulled her against him and wrapped his arms tightly around her. He stroked her back slowly, spreading tendrils of heat up and down her spine.

She rested her cheek against his shoulder. "But we weren't going to do this anymore, remember?"

"Yeah, I thought so, too," he muttered, glancing down at her. "But I changed my mind. Just this once. That okay with you?"

"Oh, yes, more than okay," she murmured, feeling at home in his well-muscled, broad-shouldered embrace. "This is nice."

"Yeah, it is," he said. After a moment, he added, "I missed you at dinner."

"Oh, Brandon," she said, blinking rapidly so he wouldn't

notice the sudden sheen of tears in her eyes brought on by his sweet words. "I didn't want to interfere in the time spent with your family."

"You wouldn't be interfering." He touched her chin and angled her face so that he was gazing into her eyes. "My family's great, but it would've been more fun if you'd been there."

Feeling ridiculously pleased, she smiled up at him. "Well, we're together now, so let's make the best of it."

"Babe," he said with a grin as he led her toward the king-size bed. "I thought you'd never ask."

Early the following morning, both Brandon and Kelly hit the ground running. The first guests began arriving at noon, excited to be a part of the highly anticipated grand opening.

The official ceremony was performed and executed with precision, flair and happy celebration. Brandon's knowledgeable sommelier stood by to pour champagne for everyone as they checked in. Wine tasting tours were recommended, hot air balloon reservations were taken and guests were whisked away to their rooms without a snag. As Brandon watched things unfold, he felt a whole new sense of pride in his employees, each of whom was in outstanding form today. So outstanding that Brandon was beginning to feel almost redundant. Strangely enough, it was a great feeling.

What added to the good vibe was the news his reservations manager had shared with him. The resort was already completely booked for the entire season. Brandon knew the Mansion would soon be recognized as the hottest destination spot in Napa Valley. And he was confident that he'd be able to walk away in a few weeks, leaving the duties of running the small, luxurious hotel to the experienced service experts he'd hired.

It was early afternoon when his mother and her two girlfriends finally arrived. Brandon met their limousine outside in the elegant *porte cochère* and ushered them into the lobby.

"Oh, it's beautiful, Brandon," Sally said as she and her friends gazed around in awe. They were all dressed in light, casual clothing and looked ready to vacation in style.

"I love the colors," Marjorie said.

He'd known his mother's two best friends, Beatrice and Marjorie, for well over twenty years. They were like favorite aunts, and Marjorie was also one of his employees. She'd headed Duke Development's human resources department for years. Now as the women strolled around the well-designed lobby, Brandon tried to see the spacious room through their eyes and concluded, not for the first time, that he was justifiably proud of what he'd accomplished here.

Brandon had been in charge of the Mansion on Silverado Trail project from day one and every decision had been his, including the design and overall concept of the place. All the rooms featured the best of California style blended, as their sales brochure stated, "with Tuscan flourishes and Provençal sensibilities."

The guest rooms were light and warm with rounded, Old World-style fireplaces and cozy hearths, terra-cotta tile floors, elegantly rustic furnishings and bold tapestries on the pale stucco walls. At one end of the wide lobby, French doors opened on to a wide terrace where colorful umbrellas shaded teak patio furniture and plush cushions. A stunning view of the vast acres of vineyards and olive groves that spread across the valley completed the picture.

"I can't wait to take the 'vine to barrel' tour," Beatrice exclaimed. "Do we get to taste the grapes as we pick them?"

"Wouldn't you rather taste the final product?" Sally asked her.

Beatrice grinned. "That, too."

"You can do it all," Brandon said. "Let's get you and your luggage settled and then you can take your pick of afternoon activities."

"I'm definitely up for wine tasting," Sally said.

"Oh, me, too," Marjorie agreed and Beatrice nodded enthusiastically.

Brandon grinned. "Then I'll show you to your suite so you can get started."

"I want to stay here forever," Marjorie cried as she turned in a circle to take in every inch of the cleverly designed and furnished two-bedroom *maison*. "All this and champagne on ice? Brandon, it's so beautiful. I'm so proud of you, and you must be proud of yourself, too."

"I'm feeling pretty good," he admitted with a chuckle. "It's nice, isn't it?"

"Nice?" Beatrice said as she opened the glass doors that led out to their private balcony. "It's glorious."

"I'm glad you think so." After showing them the button that would automatically light up the fireplace, then pointing out the secluded walkway that led to the spa facilities, Brandon headed for the door. "I'll leave you to unpack and relax. If you need anything, including me, just dial the front desk and ask."

Sally rushed over and wrapped her arms around him in a hug. "Thank you, Brandon. This is wonderful."

"You're welcome, Mom. I just want you all to relax,

pour yourselves a glass of champagne and have a great time."

His mother laughed. "Believe me, sweetie, that's exactly what we had in mind."

Two hours later, Brandon had finished up a short meeting with his brothers and the restaurant staff. Adam was on his way back to his room to check on Trish, who'd been taking a nap, while Cameron and Julia had decided to pour themselves glasses of wine and stroll through the vineyards to enjoy the sunset.

Brandon headed back to his office, but as he crossed the lobby, he spied Marjorie and Bea in the gift shop located next to the wine bar on the opposite side of the lobby from the front desk. Marjorie clutched a box of expensive chocolates and Bea held a bottle of good red wine and they were deep in conversation with the clerk. He grinned as he imagined them discussing the best wine to drink with chocolate. Glancing around, he looked for his mother, but she wasn't in the shop. A movement caught his eye and he glanced out at the terrace where Sally stood talking animatedly with Kelly.

For a brief moment, he stopped and simply enjoyed the sight of Kelly's short skirt wafting in the soft breeze and let his mind wander to what she might be wearing underneath. Another thong, he hoped, allowing himself to imagine the feel of featherlight lace against her silky—

He snapped back to reality. That was *his mother* talking to Kelly. And knowing his mother and what she was capable of in the name of matchmaking, Brandon's mood shifted immediately into suspicion. His mother and Kelly chatting? This couldn't be a good thing, so he strolled outside to put a stop to whatever mischief Sally Duke was up to.

"Hello, Mother," he said.

Sally whipped around. "Oh! Brandon, dear, you snuck up on me."

That was exactly what he'd meant to do, but he wasn't about to say so. "What were you two talking about?"

"I was just telling Kelly how marvelous she looks," Sally said. "Don't you agree?"

"Yeah, she looks great," Brandon said warily. "So what?"

Sally gave him a perplexed look. "Are you feeling all right, sweetie?"

"He's probably wondering what I'm doing away from the office," Kelly said lightly. "Which means I'd better get going. It was lovely to see you again, Mrs. Duke."

"You, too, Kelly." Sally gave her a quick hug. "I'll see you tomorrow night, if not sooner."

"I'm looking forward to it," Kelly said, then rushed through the lobby toward their offices.

"What's tomorrow night?" Brandon asked cautiously.

"Kelly's joining us for dinner."

His eyes narrowed. "Mom, what are you doing?"

"I'm not sure what you mean," she said, straightening her shoulders and meeting his gaze head-on. "Kelly does so much for all of us, I thought it would be a nice gesture to include her. My goodness, I haven't booked my own travel in over a year, thanks to her, and she helped me track down that fabulous imported baby gym for little Jake's birthday. And that's just the tip of the iceberg. She works wonders, but all that is beside the point. Kelly is simply a delightful woman and I've come to think of her as a member of our extended family. So I invited her to dinner. Frankly, I'm surprised you didn't invite her yourself."

If she only knew, Brandon thought. "Look, Mom,

Kelly's great, but that doesn't mean I want you playing matchmaker between me and her."

"Matchmaker?" She looked truly mystified, but Brandon knew for a fact that his mother was an excellent actress when she wanted to be.

He rolled his eyes at her attempt to play dumb. "You can deny it all you want, but I know you've been trying to get all of us guys married off." He folded his arms across his chest to show her he meant business. "You might've succeeded with Adam and Cameron, but you won't with me. There's no way you'll ever get me to propose to Kelly, so you might as well give up right now."

"Propose?" She blinked. "To Kelly?" She stared at him in shock for a few more seconds, then began to laugh. And she kept laughing until she was doubled over. Finally, she thumped her chest as she tried to catch her breath. "Oh, my goodness, I haven't laughed like that in years."

"And I'm sure you were laughing *with* me."

She choked on another laugh. "Of course."

"What's so damn funny, Mom?"

"Oh, honey, come on. You? Marry Kelly? That's ridiculous."

"Oh, yeah?" he said, his tone challenging as he loomed over her.

She laughed again. "Brandon sweetie, I love you dearly, but I would never do that to Kelly!"

"To *Kelly?*" Now it was Brandon's turn to be surprised. "What about me?"

"You'll survive," she said dryly, and patted his arm. "My point is, you and Kelly would be a horrible match."

"No, we wouldn't," he said, outraged, then shook his head. Damn, she was deliberately trying to trap him. "I mean, yeah, we would. I mean…what are you talking about?"

She smiled at him patiently. "Kelly is a darling girl and I would be thrilled and honored to have her as a daughter-in-law, but it's never going to happen. You two would never work out. She's too much of a romantic at heart."

"I'm not sure I agree," he said carefully. Sally had already tricked him once so he was watching every word he said.

"Yes, darling, she is," Sally said softly. "Kelly's been hurt and her heart is still tender. But that doesn't mean she's given up on love. She's still looking for a man who will truly love her. She wants the dream, Brandon. She wants to live happily ever after."

"Most women want that, I guess," he allowed, with a philosophical shrug.

"Yes, and you've made it abundantly clear that you are completely unwilling to provide any woman with that blissful scenario."

"True," he said with a rueful grin.

"So why in the world would I want to match Kelly up with you?"

His eyes narrowed. "I don't know. Why would you?"

"Exactly, I wouldn't!" she said triumphantly, effectively ending the conversation. She grabbed him in another hug, patting his back as though he were a clever four-year-old. "Now, the girls and I are going to Tra Vigne for an early dinner, so we'll catch up with you in the morning."

He watched her scurry off, wondering how in the world she'd managed to win that conversation.

Six

The grape harvest began the next morning. Guests were invited to join in as part of the complete "vine to barrel" experience, despite the fact that the Dukes employed plenty of workers to get the job done. It was a tradition for many people who vacationed in Napa Valley to take part in the harvest ritual. There was something essential and gratifying in the physical act of picking the grapes that would some day become the wine served at one's table.

"How do you know when the grapes are ready to pick?" one of the guests asked.

Brandon turned and recognized Mrs. Kingsley, who'd been one of the first to reserve a room for the harvest. This was her and her husband's first trip to Napa. Brandon stepped forward to say something, but hesitated when Kelly spoke up.

"Different winemakers have various ways of judging the readiness of the grapes," she said, reaching for a cluster of

plump grapes and severing it from the vine with her shears.
She plucked a few grapes off and handed one each to Mr.
and Mrs. Kingsley, then popped one into her own mouth.
"You can't usually taste the flavor of the finished wine in
the fruit."

The elderly woman chewed her grape. "It's very sweet."

"Yes," Kelly said. "All I can taste is the sugar. But an
expert will also taste some tannin and acidity in the skin."

Mrs. Kingsley chewed another moment, then nodded
slowly. "I see what you mean."

"There are all sorts of instruments and analyses used
to gauge the readiness of the grapes," Kelly continued.
"But I also think there's quite a lot of art mixed in with
the science. And luck, as well. After all, who knows what
the weather will bring from one season to the next?"

"So true, my dear," Mr. Kingsley said, patting his wife
on the back.

Kelly had impressed Brandon many times in the past
with both her business acumen and her social skills, and
today was no different. He watched her walking from row
to row, greeting guests, passing out bottles of water and
offering advice on everything from how to pick the fruit—
grab the large clumps of grapes rather than the individual
grapes—to counseling on the dangers of sunburn under
the warm October sun. For that problem, she would reach
into her backpack and hand out individual tubes of suntan
lotion provided by the hotel spa, as well as bright burgundy
baseball caps with the Mansion's logo emblazoned on the
front. One by one, as the guests got a look at the classy, fun
caps, everyone wanted one, and Kelly cheerfully obliged
them.

Brandon was both impressed and amused by her
resourcefulness. And apparently, so was the well-known
hotel reviewer from the national trade magazine, if

his exuberant announcement offering vineyard photo opportunities was any indication. The man pulled a small but expensive digital camera from his pocket and began shooting photographs of willing and enthusiastic guests in various stages of grape picking.

The wine-colored baseball caps had been designed to be a part of the marketing team's grand opening promotional giveaway package, but nobody had thought about using them in the vineyards to shield guests from the bright sun. Kelly deserved a bonus for that PR coup.

He made a mental note to make sure the signature caps would always be available to any guests who wanted to work or simply wander through the vineyard fields.

"She's really something," a voice said from behind Brandon.

He turned and saw his brother Adam standing nearby, also watching Kelly. "Yeah, she is."

"Maybe we should talk about promoting her to marketing or public relations."

"No way," Brandon groused. "I'm keeping her."

Intrigued, Adam lifted one eyebrow. "Keeping her?"

Brandon waved away his previous comment. "You know what I mean. Keeping her as my assistant."

"Yeah, your assistant." Adam smirked. "Right."

"What's that supposed to mean?"

"It means I don't blame you," he said, watching Kelly with new interest. "If I had someone that special working for me, I wouldn't let her go either."

"No kidding," Brandon said, knowing Trish had been hired as Adam's temporary assistant. They'd fallen in love and had married each other last year. "But we've all accepted the fact that you're a weak man."

Adam threw back his head and laughed. "Weak, huh?" Glancing around, he spied his beautiful pregnant wife sitting under the umbrella of a patio table the crew had set up earlier for guests, drinking from her water bottle. With a satisfied nod, he turned back and gave Brandon a look fraught with meaning. "It takes a strong man to recognize his own weakness."

"Whatever that means."

"I think you know what that means," he said, turning to take another look at Kelly before glancing back at Brandon.

"Nice try, bro," Brandon said, "but you're barking up the wrong tree. It's not going to happen."

"I hope you're convincing yourself because you're not convincing me."

Brandon shrugged. "I'm only convinced that you don't know what the hell you're talking about."

With a grin, Adam whacked Brandon on the back, then walked away to check on Trish, leaving Brandon to gaze over at Kelly who was still laughing and smiling and working her magic with the guests.

He scowled again as he played Adam's words over in his mind. Great. So Adam thought Brandon was falling for Kelly, while his mother had warned him that falling for Kelly was the worst thing he could do.

What was wrong with everyone in his family?

Just because he wanted Kelly as much as he wanted to take another breath, didn't mean he'd be stupid enough to propose marriage to her. Their affair was all about sex. Not marriage. Brandon didn't *do* marriage. Not now, not ever.

He shook off the serious subject matter and accepted that it was no longer just his mother he had to worry about; it was his brothers, too. Now that they were both married, they probably couldn't stand the fact that Brandon was still footloose and having a good time. In other words, he was a bachelor, unattached, single, happy. And he intended to stay that way permanently, so they would all just have to suck it up.

Meanwhile, he couldn't take his eyes off Kelly. He noticed she was wearing that glossy, berry-flavored stuff on her lips again. She'd been wearing it last night when Brandon arrived at her door after dinner. The memory of what she'd done with those sexy lips of hers made him grit his teeth with the effort it took to keep from turning rock-hard and embarrassing himself in front of his guests.

It didn't help that she wore a flimsy, feminine knit shirt that clung to her curves, along with long, dark blue jeans that showed off her world-class bottom to perfection. She'd pulled her thick, shiny hair into a flirtatious ponytail that swung back and forth, teasing him with every move she made.

If things were different, if he and Kelly were a real couple, he wouldn't hesitate to walk right over there right now and kiss her. But they weren't a real couple, and the longer he hung around staring at her, wanting her, the dumber he felt. He had plenty of work to do in his office and if he was smart, he'd leave right now and get something done. But just then, Kelly laughed, and the sweet, lighthearted sound touched and warmed some part deep within his chest, and he knew he wasn't going anywhere.

"Thanks for all your help, Kelly," Mr. Kingsley said, tipping the brim of his baseball cap toward her. "See you at the wine tasting."

"You bet, Mr. Kingsley," Kelly said, waving to the last guest and his wife as they headed out of the vineyard and back to the hotel. They both looked so cute in their matching caps as they walked away holding hands.

Kelly hadn't realized how much she would enjoy

mingling with the hotel guests. She'd never considered herself shy, but she had to admit she'd never been quite as outgoing as she'd been today. She attributed it to the newfound confidence and self-assurance she'd gained in the past week since she and Brandon had started sleeping together. And that reminded her of something else that was different about her today. She should've been utterly exhausted and ready to take a nap, but instead, she felt energized, exhilarated. How weird was that?

"Don't question it," she advised herself. "Just enjoy the feeling for as long as it lasts."

"What did you say?" Brandon said, coming up behind her.

Kelly sucked in a breath and turned around slowly to gaze up at him. He seemed taller and broader somehow, but maybe that was because she'd worn low-heeled boots today instead of high heels. Or maybe it was because he looked so gorgeous and larger than life in his rugged denim shirt and blue jeans instead of a suit and tie. Whatever the reason, she had to stop staring like a fool and answer the simple question he'd asked her.

"I was just talking to myself," she muttered, then forced herself to smile casually. "Wasn't this a fun day? I think everyone enjoyed themselves."

"Thanks to you," he said with a teasing grin. "My brothers want to give you a bonus and promote you to head of marketing for coming up with the idea to pass out suntan lotion and baseball caps to the guests."

"Oh, that was just a spur of the moment thing," she insisted, but her smile broadened at the compliment. "When I saw the weather report and realized how warm it was going to be, I grabbed a few caps on the way out, just in case. Then when everyone seemed to want one, I ran back and got more. Same goes for the suntan lotion."

"Well, thank you for thinking ahead," he said, slinging a friendly arm around her as they walked. "It really paid off."

The praise, together with his touch, made her feel as warm and cozy as a happy cat. She had the strongest urge to wrap herself around his legs and purr contentedly, but she managed to control herself.

"I understand you're joining us for dinner," Brandon said as they left the vineyard and walked along the flower-lined brick path back to the hotel.

She glanced at him sideways. "I hope that's okay with you."

"Of course it's okay. My mother considers you a part of the family. We'll have a good time. Even though we'll have to keep our hands off each other."

"I guess we can manage that for an hour or two," she said, laughing softly. "I really like your mom."

"That makes two of us," he said, squeezing her shoulder companionably.

Purr, she thought to herself, and snuggled against him, wanting to be wrapped up in his warmth for as long as it lasted.

"A toast to the Mansion at Silverado Trail," Adam said, raising his wineglass.

The rest of the Duke family, along with Beatrice and Marjorie and Kelly, raised their glasses to meet his.

"To the Mansion," Cameron echoed.

"Long may it reign as the supreme destination among all the Duke properties," Brandon said with a grin.

Adam chuckled. "In Napa Valley anyway."

"Yeah," Cameron said. "Can't compete with Monarch Dunes."

"Or Fantasy Mountain," Adam added.

"They're all fabulous properties," Marjorie said. "You men have done an incredible job. I'm so proud of you."

"Thanks, Marjorie," Adam said. "But it's partly your fault for making sure we hire only the best people."

"Like Kelly and Trish, for instance," Cameron said, grinning as he raised his glass to both women.

"Ah, yes," Marjorie said, winking at Trish. "I'm glad you've finally recognized the true genius behind Duke Development."

"Since you were the one who hired Kelly and Trish, I would have to agree," Brandon said, his gaze sweeping over Kelly.

Kelly felt her cheeks heating and rushed to change the subject. Turning to Julia, she asked, "Did you enjoy your massage today?"

"Oh, it was heavenly." She looked across the table at Brandon. "I hope you're paying Ingrid, the masseuse, a lot of money. She's worth her weight in gold."

"That's what I like to hear," Brandon said with a firm nod.

Trish pursed her lips in thought. "A massage every day is so civilized, don't you agree."

Kelly laughed. "I really do."

"Absolutely," Beatrice chimed in.

Since there were nine of them, Brandon had reserved the small but elegant private room next to the wine cellar for their dinner. When they first arrived, he'd pulled Kelly's chair out for her and as she'd begun to sit down, he'd let his hand glide from the small of her back up to her neck. Shivers ran through her and she almost gasped from the provocative touch. He'd flashed her a very private, very wicked grin as he took his seat.

They'd all chosen to dine off the tasting menu, that meant a different wine with each course. The food was delicious and the pairings were perfect. Kelly savored each delicate bite and every sip of the outstanding wines. Everyone agreed that the kitchen staff had outdone themselves.

She found the conversations that circled the table to be fascinating and enjoyable. Sally and Marjorie teased Beatrice about some of the men she'd met through her online dating service, urging Beatrice to describe a few of her funnier moments.

Julia talked about the trials and tribulations of turning her massive family estate into an art museum and learning center for children, complete with vegetable garden and petting zoo. She regaled them with stories about the monkey that entertained the kids by riding the goat, and the new zookeeper she'd hired who wanted to give falconry lessons.

As Julia spoke, Cameron reached for her hand and tucked it into his. Kelly found herself both captivated and wistful, looking at the way he gazed at Julia. Both of Brandon's brothers were deeply in love with their wives and weren't afraid to let their feelings show. Was it too much for Kelly to hope that, some day, a man would look at her that way?

A few minutes later, as their first course dishes were cleared, she happened to glance at Brandon who was laughing at something his brother Adam had said. As if he sensed her looking his way, Brandon turned his head and his gaze locked on to hers. The heat was instant, powerful and profound. Her breath caught in her throat and her heart fluttered. Her vision fogged, then narrowed to a point where only Kelly and Brandon existed together in the room. Sounds and voices ceased to be anything more than a mild buzzing in her ears.

Seconds later, she blinked, and just as quickly, Brandon

turned away as though he hadn't experienced the same lightning bolt moment. As though nothing monumental had just occurred between the two of them. So why was her heart still beating too fast? Why had her appetite suddenly vanished?

Kelly would've sworn in that moment that Brandon had looked at her with the same level of intensity and love she'd seen in his brothers' eyes when they gazed at their wives. Had she imagined it? Was she going crazy?

She glanced around to see if anyone else had noticed her sudden discomfiture, but everyone, including Brandon, was talking and laughing, carrying on conversations, sipping their wine and reaching for bread as they'd been doing since the meal began.

She'd clearly misconstrued his look, and the realization made her feel like a lovesick idiot. It had just been wishful thinking, probably because only minutes before, she'd been mooning over the soulful way Cameron had been gazing at Julia.

She reached for her water glass and took a long sip. Then she ordered herself to breathe evenly and resolved to forget what she thought she'd just seen, brushing it off as an inane figment of her imagination.

"You didn't eat much at dinner tonight," Brandon said later that night after they'd made love. They were stretched out on her bed, facing each other, and his hand rested on her arm.

"My first course was so much more filling than I thought it would be," Kelly said, and cursed herself for lying. "But everything I tasted was wonderful. Jean Pierre has a megahit on his hands."

"I think so, too. And I received a number of compliments about you today, too."

"Me?"

"Yes, you," he said, moving closer as he began to slide his hand up and down her back in slow, sensual strokes. "The guests appreciated the way you helped out in the vineyards today. You were a regular social director out there, making sure everyone had whatever they needed and showing the guests how to harvest the grapes. Where did you learn how to do that?"

She sighed as his hand grazed her shoulder, causing little tingles of excitement to surge through her system. "Sometimes I walk through the vineyards on my lunch hour, so I've gotten to know some of the guys who work there. They showed me how to do it."

"Really?" He reached over and swept a strand of hair off her forehead. "Well, you're obviously a natural. If you ever want a job in the vineyard, you just let me know."

She smiled. "I'm sure the perks are enticing. All the wine I can drink?"

"That's right. As long as you pick the grapes and crush them, you can drink all the wine you want."

"I'm kind of a lightweight drinker," she said, "so I'm not sure all that hard work would be worth it."

"But wait, you'd get to wear that really cool hat."

She laughed. "Now you're talking my language."

"Yeah?" He tugged her closer and rolled until she was straddling him.

Her laughter faded and she splayed her hands against his firm chest. "Brandon, our ground rules have gone out the window again."

"You noticed that, too?"

"I did," she said, smiling to hide the sadness she felt. "I think we need to accept the fact that this will be our last night together."

He covered her hands with his. "Do you think so?"

"We're both getting so busy," she added lamely, "and your family's here now."

"Yeah," he said. "And we can't forget that the clown-who-shall-not-be-named will be here in a day or two."

Kelly sighed. She'd been so anxious to carry out her Roger plan, but now the thought of seeing him was simply depressing.

"Tell you what," Brandon said, tapping her chin so that she looked up and met his gaze. "Tomorrow is hours away yet, so for now, let's forget about the world outside this room."

She moaned in pleasure as he lifted her up and onto his solid length. "Oh, that feels so good."

"Now you're talking *my* language," he murmured, and proceeded to please her in every way possible.

A long while later, as Brandon held her in his arms, Kelly tried to commit to memory every sensual feeling she'd experienced tonight. This would be the last time they ever made love with each other, and she wanted to remember the heat of his skin against hers, the weight of his leg on her thigh, his manly scent, the taste and pressure of his lips when he'd kissed her so thoroughly.

She thought back to the dinner with his family earlier tonight and the lovely feeling of warmth and inclusiveness she'd felt. She remembered that moment when Brandon looked at her with all the intensity of a man in love. Oh, maybe it wasn't real, maybe she'd imagined it, maybe she was a fool. But she would never forget how, for those few sweet moments, she'd felt like a woman who was loved by Brandon Duke.

The following morning, Brandon left her room before dawn. Kelly found it impossible to drift back to sleep and eventually tossed the covers aside and sat up. Today was the day, she thought, and mustered every last ounce of resolve she had within her. It was time to accept the unhappy fact that she and Brandon had just spent their last night together.

Climbing out of bed, she made her way to the shower. Today was Sunday and Brandon would spend the day with his family. He'd rented a limousine to take them all on a champagne tour of the valley. It would be fun for everyone, but it was partly a business excursion as well, because he and his brothers had discussed going into partnership with one of the champagne vintners. Last night, he'd been sweet enough to ask Kelly to join them, but she'd demurred. Since they'd decided to bring their delicious affair to an end, it would be awkward for her to spend more than the minimum amount of time required around Brandon.

Tomorrow, Monday, was the day Roger and others from his hedge fund company would check into the Mansion. They would be here for five long days. So besides having to deal with the countless other demands of her job, Kelly would have to deal with her ex-boyfriend.

But that was exactly the way she wanted it to be. She had no intention of calling off her plan to get even with Roger. This small act of revenge was all she'd thought about and worked toward for the past few months. It would bring her much needed closure and allow her to move forward in her life with confidence and a new sense of assurance that she was a strong woman in charge of her own life. Strong enough to take those first daunting steps into the dating arena where she hoped to find a good, decent man who would cherish her as much as she would cherish him.

But because of what she hoped to accomplish with the Roger Plan, she and Brandon had agreed to put an end to their romantic evenings together. It was bad enough that they'd vowed to end things when his family arrived—only to handily break that vow in their rush to make love again. Breaking their ground rules simply couldn't happen again.

For one thing, it wasn't fair to Brandon to use him the way she had been using him. In the beginning, she'd begged him for help in the area of romance and seduction and he'd agreed. At this point, he had more than lived up to his end of the bargain.

And for another thing, it couldn't be healthy for her to keep pretending that the two of them had any sort of loving, caring relationship beyond the walls of their office. No, outside of the office, all they had between them was a few long nights of mutually satisfying sex.

Satisfying? As she blew her hair dry, Kelly couldn't help but roll her eyes. *Satisfying* was putting it mildly. What they'd had was a firestorm of passionate, hot, wild, electrifying jungle sex. Whew. She was getting hot just thinking about it. She turned off the hair dryer and patted her wrists with a damp towel. As she dried off, she thought about last night, their final evening together. It had been memorable, to say the least.

Despite losing her appetite during dinner, Kelly was glad she'd been able to bounce back after that one odd, surreal moment when she'd thought she'd seen true emotion in Brandon's eyes. She laughed at herself now, recalling that she'd definitely managed to rally when her favorite chocolate soufflé dessert was placed in front of her.

She'd honestly enjoyed herself with Brandon and his family and his mom's friends. They all shared so much love for each other. It was obvious they enjoyed laughing and teasing each other, telling jokes and sharing old family stories with anyone who was new to the group. It was lovely to hear about Sally's latest victories in tracking down her husband's family members.

As they all left the restaurant and walked back to their rooms, Kelly realized she hadn't had that much fun in years.

Brandon's two sisters-in-law, Trish and Julia, were sweet, funny and smart, and they'd generously welcomed her into their small circle. She'd felt an instant camaraderie with both of them.

And she didn't mind admitting that she was already half in love with Sally Duke. There was no one more gracious and friendly than Brandon's mother. She and her girlfriends, Bea and Marjorie, giggled like teenagers and always managed to have the best time together. Kelly had to admire the three women, who'd staunchly maintained such a strong friendship throughout their lives.

Brandon's brothers were officially her employers, but that hadn't kept them from acting like her own big brothers with their good-natured teasing and clever banter.

After she and Brandon returned to her room for the night, their lovemaking had run the gamut of emotions for both of them. By turns he'd been sweet, funny, passionate, tender, erotic and completely breathtaking. Perhaps it was due to the fact that they both knew this would be their last night together, but it seemed as if their lovemaking had reached a new level of passion and heat. The night had been wonderful and she would never forget it. What woman in her right mind wouldn't hold those memories in her heart forever?

On the other hand, what woman in her right mind would look at Brandon Duke's magnificent naked body and tell him their affair was over? Was there a woman in the world who was that strong?

So maybe she was crazy for insisting they end their

affair now. But on the off chance that Brandon showed up at her door tonight, thinking he could break their ground rules once again, she would have no choice but to turn him away. It was the best thing for both of them. This time, she would have to be firm. They had no future together, except in business. Their fleeting love affair was over.

"He won't care," she whispered. Why was she making such a big deal about it? Brandon attracted women like flies to honey. For goodness' sake, the man had his own gravitational pull! He would have some new woman in his bed in the time it took Kelly to say "Bye-bye."

As she brushed her teeth, she forced herself to recall the many women Brandon had dated and broken up with in the past. She thought of the numerous diamond bracelets she'd purchased, just so he could give his date of the month a lovely parting gift before he kissed her goodbye for the last time.

The last thing Kelly wanted was her very own diamond bracelet from Brandon. Dear God, she would die of humiliation if he tried to give her one as he held the door open for her to leave.

That settled it. There was no way she would ever allow herself to remain in a relationship that was guaranteed to end in such a pathetic, clichéd fashion.

No, her long-range plans to fall in love and get married had to be her overriding single focus from now on.

"He'll follow the rules this time," she murmured as she slipped on a pair of yoga pants and a sleeveless T-shirt. After all, Brandon had been reluctant to get involved with her from the beginning. Oh, he'd been more than reluctant; he had absolutely refused to help her. Of course, he'd obviously changed his mind and she had to admit he'd definitely warmed up to the task. *In more ways than one,* she thought, as a sudden image of his clever hands and mouth on her most intimate parts flashed through her mind.

"Oh, God." With a shake of her head, she calculated that she would only have to suffer from these erotic flashbacks for the next few decades or so. Forcing the images away, she quickly tied her sneakers, grabbed her purse and a light jacket and left the room to do her weekly shopping and errands.

Monday morning, Kelly was seated at her desk bright and early, determined to be the proficient and talented assistant Brandon had hired in the first place—and nothing more. She felt fully rested for the first time in a week and as she made a second pot of coffee, she marveled that she'd actually been able to sleep through the night. She'd worried at first that she'd become so used to sleeping curled up next to Brandon's warmth that she would no longer be able to sleep on her own. But as soon as her head hit the pillow, she'd fallen into an exhausted slumber and when she woke up this morning, she was surprised to realize she'd slept straight through the night.

It helped that Brandon had stayed out late with his brothers and a potential new partner the night before. When he called her on his way back to the hotel, just to say good-night, she'd cut the conversation short, claiming to be half asleep.

Another reason she was grateful for a good's night sleep was because today was the day that Roger would arrive. Kelly would need every ounce of her brainpower to concentrate on him. Earlier, in her room, she'd spent way too long on her hair and makeup and wardrobe choices. But she was glad she'd taken the time, glad she'd chosen the elegant blue-and-white swirly wrap dress that accentuated her narrow waist and curves, because when

Brandon walked into the office this morning and saw her, his eyes had lit up and he'd grinned wolfishly. That was exactly the reaction she'd been hoping for, and it made her feel all warm and glowing inside. Brandon's appreciative gaze had infused her with all the confidence she would need to stand up to Roger this afternoon.

The telephone rang and Kelly answered it immediately.

"Let me speak to Brandon," an imperious female voice demanded.

Kelly's lips twisted in a grimace. Bianca Stephens again. She'd grudgingly given Brandon the woman's message last week, but she had no idea if he'd returned the call.

"Just a moment, please," she murmured, and put the woman on hold. Pressing the intercom button, she announced the call to Brandon.

There was a pause, then Brandon said, "Take a message, would you please, Kelly? I don't have time to talk to her right now."

"All right." Kelly stared at the telephone, knowing the woman wouldn't take the news well. She composed herself, then muttered, "Ah well, here goes nothing," and pressed another button. "I'm sorry, Ms. Stephens, but Brandon is unable to take your call right now. May I give him a message?"

"You must be kidding."

"No, ma'am, I'm not. He's unavailable, so I'll have to take a message for him."

"Fine, I have a message for him," she said heatedly. "Tell him he needs to fire his receptionist, or whoever the hell you are, because you are simply incompetent."

Kelly gasped. "I…I beg your pardon?"

"You didn't hear me? So now you're deaf, too?"

"No, I'm not deaf, but—"

"Then put me through to Brandon now."

"I don't think so," Kelly said, and quickly disconnected the call. Shaking, she jumped up from her desk and paced back and forth, pressing her hands to her cheeks as she shook her head in numb disbelief. Had she actually hung up on someone her boss considered a friend? Yes, she had! On the other hand, she couldn't believe Brandon was actually friends with such a horrible person.

Was it too soon to take another vacation? She must be under more pressure than she'd realized if she'd actually hung up on someone.

How would she explain her actions to Brandon? She had to say something. He would hear about it eventually from the rude queen bee herself. With one last shake of her head, she slid back into her chair and tried to dream up a reasonable explanation.

Brandon breathed deeply in relief as he watched the red light on the phone disappear, signaling that the call was disconnected.

Bianca had phoned last week and he'd never returned her call, and now he'd just refused to talk to her again. He'd never been someone who avoided confrontation, and, hell, Bianca had always been good for some laughs. She'd also made herself available to him countless times and was always up for a hearty round of purely casual sex whenever they were in the same part of the country. So why hadn't he taken the call? What was his problem?

He dug his fingers through his hair, trying to figure it out. Bianca rarely made demands on his time, only calling when she was on the West Coast and wanted to get together for the aforementioned casual sex.

But unfortunately, he reasoned, right now wasn't a good time for him to see her. No, right now, it was important that Brandon make himself available for Kelly and help her get through this difficult time with that idiot Roger. So yeah, that's why he couldn't see Bianca. That was his excuse. He was being Mr. Helpful. That was just the kind of guy he was.

His intercom rang and he picked up the phone. "Yes, Kelly?"

She spoke in a rush. "I wanted to let you know that I accidentally dropped Ms. Stephens's call and she might be a bit angry with me. I know you don't have time to speak with her right now, but would you like me to get her back on the line and explain what happened?"

"Don't bother, she'll get over it," he said. "I'll call her next week."

"All right," she said, sounding relieved. "Thank you."

He hung up the phone, sat back in his chair and stared out the window. Maybe he would call Bianca next week and maybe he wouldn't. To be honest, Bianca had never been someone he'd call "fun." Her world revolved around herself, her job, her problems, her triumphs, her own importance. In other words, she talked about herself all the time. Yes, he'd always found her mildly amusing when she bitched about the people who ran her television network, the people she worked with, the people who came on her show. She was always complaining about something or other.

He didn't need that kind of aggravation right now. He had to concentrate his energy on watching—and possibly "helping"—Kelly complete her warped plan to get Roger back.

And he had to focus on keeping his hands to himself. She'd made it clear two nights ago that he wasn't allowed to break their ground rules again. He might have to revisit that decision sometime in the near future, but not while Roger was here. That didn't mean he would leave Kelly alone, though. He wasn't about to let her get hurt implementing her crazy plan.

Today was the day Roger the schmuck would be arriving. Brandon smacked his hands together in anticipation of finally meeting face to face the jerk who'd made Kelly's life so miserable.

Let the games begin.

Seven

"Perhaps you don't understand just who you're dealing with," said a cool blonde woman standing at the registration desk. An elegantly dressed man stood nearby, tapping his well-shod foot impatiently.

Kelly would know that foot tapper anywhere, even with his back to her. It was Roger, of course. Watching him now, she recalled that any small inconvenience often sent him into an emotional tailspin. The first warning sign was the foot tapping.

Gathered around the lobby were the rest of Roger's group, ten or twelve businessmen and several women, all waiting to check in.

Sharon, the front desk clerk, smiled warmly. "We're all well aware of Mr. Hempstead, and we're happy and honored to welcome him and his associates to the Mansion on Silverado Trail. We're so pleased that your company has chosen our resort for your retreat. We've arranged for

Mr. Hempstead to stay in *Sauvignon,* our most deluxe
and private *maison* suite. I'm just finishing up with his
paperwork and I'll take care of the rest of your people
right away."

"I certainly hope so."

Sharon's smile never faded as she slid two plastic suite
cards inside a sturdy cardboard case and touched the shiny
brass bell on the counter. A clear chime rang out. "One of
our bellmen will be here momentarily to accompany Mr.
Hempstead to his suite. I can show you where it is on our
map."

"Don't bother," the woman said frostily. "Just book me
into the room nearest Mr. Hempstead's."

Kelly studied the woman curiously and assumed she
was Roger's assistant or an associate of some kind. She
was attractive in a cold-blooded sort of way. Her black
pinstriped designer suit and gray silk shirt seemed overly
businesslike and out of place in the casually elegant lobby,
but Kelly had to admit that the look suited the woman. She
didn't come across as the casual type.

The thought suddenly occurred to Kelly that this woman
and Roger might be sleeping together. That could pose a
problem, one Kelly hadn't even considered.

She shifted her gaze back to Roger. He was still very
good-looking, naturally, but she noticed that his dark blond
hair was beginning to thin on top. He looked unnaturally
tan and she wondered if he'd taken to visiting a tanning
salon. His brown suit was impeccable, of course, but
slightly dated, at least by West Coast standards. His striped
tie showed off his beloved burgundy and gold college
colors. He looked exactly like what he was: the spoiled,
privileged scion of a venerable East Coast family.

At that moment, Sharon glanced around with a mildly
anxious expression on her face, and Kelly knew it was time

to defuse the situation. But just as she started to approach Roger, Brandon entered the lobby from the opposite doorway. He walked right up to Roger as Kelly watched in fear and horror.

"Hello, Mr. Hempstead," Brandon said spiritedly, grabbing Roger's hand, shaking it with enthusiasm. "It's a pleasure to meet you. We've been looking forward to your visit for quite some time. I'm Brandon Duke. Welcome to the Mansion on Silverado Trail."

"Thanks," Roger said, clearly impressed that the former NFL quarterback and billionaire hotel mogul had singled him out. "We've heard good buzz about the place, but there must've been a mix-up because our rooms…"

"Not a mix-up," Brandon said quickly, shaking his finger for emphasis. "An upgrade."

Kelly frowned. What in the world was he up to?

The differences between the two men were blatantly clear to Kelly now, and she couldn't believe she'd ever told Brandon they were similar. Yes, they were both wealthy, Type A and driven to succeed. But she had also called Brandon arrogant. Yes, he was bossy and wanted to have things his way, but now, as she watched him converse with Roger, she could see that Brandon didn't have one iota of the haughty arrogance that her former boyfriend had.

As the men continued to talk, the cool blonde turned around and eyed Brandon from head to toe as if he were a succulent steak and she a hungry lioness.

She'd seen enough. Kelly straightened her shoulders and shook her hair back, then walked briskly toward the front desk.

"Hello, Roger," she said.

Roger looked at her with mild disinterest, then did a double take and his eyes goggled. "Kelly?"

"Yes, Roger, it's me." She circled around to the other

side of the counter. "Now, let's get you registered and off to your rooms, shall we?"

"You work here?" Roger said, unblinking.

"I certainly do," she said, and accompanied the words with what she hoped was an alluring smile. "Welcome to the Mansion on Silverado Trail. Let me see what I can do to speed up the registration process."

Just then, Michael, the other registration clerk, came rushing over. "Thanks, Kelly. I can take over now." He leaned closer and whispered, "I had to change all their restaurant reservations. They brought two extra people with no notice."

It figured that Roger would do something to botch up the works, Kelly thought, but she said nothing as she rounded the counter.

Brandon stepped up beside her and smiled genially to the crowd. "Ladies and gentlemen, Michael and Sharon will have you settled as quickly as possible. I'd like to extend my wishes for a pleasant stay, and hope you'll all enjoy the complimentary champagne basket our catering staff will be delivering to your rooms within the next half hour."

There were smiles and a chorus of thanks from several in the group, but Roger ignored all of it.

"Kelly?" He took hold of her arm and pulled her aside. "I hardly recognized you. It's been a long time. How have you been?"

"I've been wonderful, Roger. How about you?"

He ignored the question and continued to stare. "You look fantastic. What have you done with yourself?"

"Oh, nothing special," she said nonchalantly as she fluffed her hair. "I cut my hair."

"It's more than that," he said, frowning. "There's something else…"

"Oh, you know, I work out, eat right, drink great wine." She beamed a confident smile at him. "Life is good."

"Well, whatever you're doing, it's working," he said raptly, and leaned in close. "Listen, are you free tonight? We could have dinner."

"Tonight? No, I'm afraid—"

"She's busy," Brandon said abruptly, looming directly behind her. "She has to work late."

Kelly turned and stabbed him with a pointed look that clearly said *buzz off.* Then she turned back to Roger and smiled tightly. "Yes, unfortunately, I'm working tonight, but I'm free Thursday night. Are you?"

"Yes," he said immediately. "We'll have dinner."

"Wait a minute," Brandon muttered.

Kelly elbowed him in the stomach discreetly.

"Oww," he said under his breath.

She ignored him and continued to focus her energy on her ex-boyfriend. "I've got to get back to my office, Roger, but I'm sure I'll run into you around the resort between now and Thursday. I hope you all have a wonderful visit."

Roger raised one eyebrow rakishly. "Oh, I'll definitely see you around."

"So that's Roger," Brandon said as they strolled back to the office together.

Kelly stopped and planted her hands on her hips. "And what did you think you were doing, butting in like that?"

"Hey, I did you a favor."

"You said you wouldn't say anything to him."

"I was being my charming hotelier self. Extending an open hand to one of our *important* guests."

"Open fist, you mean."

He snorted. "Don't tempt me. Guy's a real snake oil salesman, isn't he?"

She shook her head as they continued walking. "He's not that bad."

"Yeah, he is," Brandon countered. "And who's the ice queen?"

"That woman with him?" Kelly frowned. "I just assumed she was his assistant, but she was awfully pushy, wasn't she?"

He glanced at her sideways. "Yeah, kind of like you."

"I'm not pushy," she said in mock outrage.

"Yeah, you are," he said as he led her into their office suite and closed and locked the door.

"Well, I guess I can be pushy once in a while, but I'm nothing like—"

Without warning, he spun her around. She let out a tiny shriek as he urged her back against the wall.

"Just look at the way you push me around," Brandon said. "The way you force me to do this…" He lowered his head and began to nibble her neck. Kelly felt the electric sensation all the way down to her toes.

It had only been two days. But oh, how she had missed him.

"And this…" Brandon used both hands to flip her short jacket off her shoulders, trapping her arms behind her and causing her breasts to be thrust forward.

"But…oh, yes."

"So damn pushy." He quickly unknotted the thin ties that held her dress together and reached for her breasts.

"Brandon," she whispered, then moaned when he swiftly maneuvered her bra out of the way and used his fingers to tease and excite her nipples. But through the thick haze of pleasure, she remembered something important and grabbed his hand. "Brandon, wait. We weren't going to do this anymore. We should stop. We should…"

"We'll stop after this, I swear," he muttered. "But I can't stop. I've got to have you now."

"Yes, please," she said, straining to remove her jacket as he bent to lick her breasts. "Hurry."

"Pushy," he murmured again as he kissed and nibbled his way back and forth between her breasts.

"Oh, shut up and kiss me," she grumbled as she reached up and whipped his jacket off.

His laugh was deep and full. "I do love a pushy woman."

Then his lips covered hers in an openmouthed kiss and his tongue swept inside to tangle with hers. Through the mindless haze of passion, Kelly's hands fumbled with his belt, finally undoing it and pulling it loose. She unbuttoned his pants, then started on his zipper, easing it down over his burgeoning erection.

In the back of her brain, she registered the words he'd said, *I do love a pushy woman,* but knew he didn't mean anything by it. It was just something he'd said in the heat of the moment. She wouldn't make more of him using the word "love" than that. Otherwise, she'd go crazy overthinking every word he'd ever said.

Seconds later, Brandon made her forget to think at all as he took first one nipple, then the other, into his mouth, sucking and licking until she thought she would die of sheer pleasure.

He yanked her dress off her shoulders and watched it fall to the floor, revealing the black thong she wore.

"Whoa."

She boldly kicked the dress away, then leaned back against the wall. "Do you like it?"

He simply stared at her for several long moments, taking in every inch of her, from her hair down to her feet. "I recall telling you it was my personal choice."

"I do recall you mentioning it."

His smile was slow and wicked. "The heels are a nice touch, too."

"Why, thank you."

"Damn, you're incredible," he whispered, skimming his hands down the outside of her thighs as he knelt in front of her.

"Brandon, what…"

"Shh, let me have you," he said, gently moving her legs apart to allow him to kiss the inside skin of her thighs, starting above her knee and moving up, up, until he reached her heated core.

"So beautiful," he murmured.

She was incapable of speech as he cupped his hands around her bottom, angled her toward him and feasted. He took his time, lavishing kisses and strokes of his clever tongue everywhere, touching her, urging her up, closer and closer to the peak of oblivion, only to ease back, teasing her, playing her until she was ready to scream.

"Brandon, please," she cried.

"Soon, love," he promised.

"Now." It had to be now or she would die from need.

He moved then, his mouth trailing kisses across her stomach, then up and over her breasts as he stood once again.

She opened her eyes and looked into his, saw the tender passion reflected there and knew in that moment that he felt the same way she did. It was more than simple need or wanting. She couldn't name it, could only feel it, deep in her bones. It flowed through her bloodstream, filling her with an age-old understanding, warming her down into her soul. He felt it, too. She knew it, saw it in his eyes. That stunning awareness filled her with joy as he kissed her lips and met her need with his own.

With no effort at all, he lifted her up and turned so that

he now leaned against the wall with her in his arms. She wrapped her legs around his waist and moaned as he eased her onto his firm erection, filling her completely.

"Yes," he uttered, kissing her, his mouth taking hold of hers in an explosion of heat and pleasure. Together they pushed each other to the limit, then slowed, unwilling to bring an end to the ecstasy. They moved together in a deliberate, unhurried rhythm, until the passion built again and he pumped into her until she couldn't catch her breath. But she didn't care, it didn't matter. He was all she wanted, all she'd been waiting for. He moved with an urgency that matched her own, bringing them back to that edge where they teetered for an instant, then drove themselves over in a climax so all-consuming, so shattering, she wondered if they would survive the fall.

"What just happened here?" Kelly asked, her voice betraying her dazed and confused state.

Brandon nudged her with his foot. "You forced me to have my way with you, remember?"

She tried to work up the energy to smack his leg, but there was no power behind it and she ended up merely grazing his skin with her fingertips.

"So much for ground rules," she said under her breath as she took in the unbelievable scene. Somehow, they'd staggered over to the office couch where they were now sprawled at either end in various stages of undress. Clothing was scattered across the floor. Kelly had grabbed the colorful shawl that was draped over the back of the couch to cover herself, but it didn't do much good. Brandon was gloriously naked. The sight reminded her of some decadent tableau painting.

"Come here," Brandon said, grabbing her ankle and tugging her closer, then pulling her up to sit on his lap.

Kelly wrapped her arms around his middle and allowed herself a moment to cuddle with him and feel cherished.

"Now what were you saying about ground rules?" he said.

"Oh, nothing."

"Well then," he said, taking her at her word as he combed his fingers lazily through her hair. "How about if we get dressed and go grab some dinner?"

But she knew what she had to do.

It was now or never. Breathing in deeply, filling her lungs with fortifying air, she let it all out slowly as she gathered her wits. Then, before she could change her mind, she blurted, "Brandon, we have to stop doing that."

He leaned his head over to meet her gaze. "Stop doing what? Eating dinner?"

"I'm serious."

"About eating?" he asked, stroking her back. "Me, too. I'm starving."

"Brandon."

She could feel his lips curve in a smile as he kissed the top of her head. Then he said, "Yes, Kelly?"

"You know what I'm talking about." She reached to take hold of his hand for strength. "We have to stop, you know, breaking the rules, having sex."

"Do we?"

"You know we do." She stared solemnly into his eyes as she squeezed his firm hand. "We talked about it before. We were supposed to stop when your family got here."

"That didn't work," he said.

"No kidding."

He chuckled and kissed her shoulder.

"Then we said we'd stop when Roger arrived," Kelly said, stretching her neck to allow his mouth to roam her skin. "And now he's here, and look at us."

"Yes, just look at us," he said, and lifted her hair to run more kisses along her neckline.

She could barely speak, but knew she had to say what was on her mind. "You've been so generous to help me with all of this. We've been together almost every night for a week and it's been wonderful. I'm having the most amazing time of my life." Her eyelashes fluttered and she looked away, not wanting him to see the confusion and pain she knew was so close to the surface. "But now we should stop before we get…"

He tipped her chin up gently to get a better look at her. "Before we get…what, Kelly?"

Before we get involved. Before you get tired of me, she thought, but didn't say aloud. Instead, she ruffled his hair lightly with her hands and said, "Before we get caught by the housekeeping staff."

Brandon knew he should be glad that she was calling him out on breaking the ground rules—again. He knew they had to finally end their affair.

So why was he so eager to change her mind?

She was right, they definitely needed to pull back—to stop. After all, he knew their affair had been temporary to begin with, and the last thing he wanted to do was jeopardize their working relationship.

But gazing at Kelly now, he also knew there was something else happening here that he wasn't ready to give up on. It was hard to explain, but she touched him on a level that he hadn't known existed before. It wasn't just the sex, although sex with Kelly was incendiary, to put it mildly. No, it was more than just sex. He *liked* her, damn it, and he wanted to be with her. When they weren't together, he missed her. The feeling wouldn't last; it never did. He knew that much. But as long as they were having a good time now, why should they call it quits and be miserable when they could keep seeing each other and be happy?

Ultimately, Brandon knew he would never be the man she needed him to be. His mother had been right about that. Kelly was the type of woman who was made for love and marriage. For family. Real family. The kind of family he knew nothing about.

Yes, it was true that Sally had saved him all those years ago, and together with Adam and Cameron, the four of them had formed a strong family bond. But until Sally came along, all Brandon had ever known of family life was misery. And that kind of memory stayed with a man. Haunted him. Reminded him that he would never be able to live up to the ideal man he saw reflected in Kelly's eyes.

But that didn't mean they couldn't enjoy each other for as long as it lasted.

"Look," he said, stroking the hair back from her face and resting his hand on her neck. "Maybe it's crazy, but I don't want to stop seeing you. I'm having a great time. And you're enjoying yourself, too, aren't you?"

She smiled and reached over to touch his cheek. "Yes, of course. You know I am."

"Then for now, that's all that matters." And to settle it, he pulled her close and met her lips with his.

Eight

Kelly poked her head inside Brandon's office the next morning. "I'm running these invoices over to the concierge desk. Do you need anything while I'm out?"

"No, thanks," Brandon mouthed and waved her off as he was still wrapped up in a phone call with the lawyers.

As she strolled along the sun-kissed terrace that led toward the lobby, Kelly thought about the night before. She and Brandon had snuck out of the hotel together and driven into St. Helena for the best cheeseburger and French fries she'd ever tasted in her life. Maybe it was the company, but she couldn't remember ever having a better time. They'd laughed and shared stories as though they were a real couple out on a real date. But it hadn't been a real date and they weren't a real couple. They were just enjoying sex and the occasional dinner out.

"But isn't that what dating is all about?" Kelly murmured aloud. "Sex and dinner?" After all, if someone were watching them, they would've thought she and Brandon were a normal young couple in love.

But they weren't in love. Far from it.

But so what? Last night, Brandon had said he was having a great time with her, so why not keep it going? Where was the harm in that?

"We're having fun," Kelly insisted to herself as she turned onto the flower-lined brick walkway that circled the main building housing the lobby, then added to her own conscience, "So back off."

"Kelly?"

"Oh." She'd been wrapped up in her thoughts, paying no attention to where she was going and suddenly, Roger stood a mere three feet in front of her. "Hello, Roger. What are you up to this morning?"

He pointed in the direction of the spa. "We've taken over the Pavilion for the day to conduct some team-building exercises."

The Pavilion was a large, open-beamed cottage used for special occasions, weddings, dinners and small conferences. Secluded, private, it was situated beyond the spa in the midst of old growth olive trees and towering oaks. It was one of Kelly's favorite secret places on the property.

"Oh, how interesting," she said politely. "I hope it's a successful exercise."

He stepped a few inches closer and took hold of her elbow in an intimate gesture. "Listen, Kelly, I've been thinking about you all night. I've really missed you. Do you think we could—"

"Roger?" a female voice called out. "Are you coming?"

Kelly turned and saw the ice queen approaching. Today she wore a severe black suit with a crisp gray blouse and five-inch, patent-leather black heels. She looked like Della the Dominatrix, minus the leather whip.

"Hello, Ariel," Roger said. He didn't sound thrilled to see her.

"We can't start without you," she said, shielding her eyes from the sunshine.

She was pretty, Kelly thought, except for two unfortunate vertical lines between her eyebrows that dug in deep when she was aggravated, which seemed to be her permanent state. The lines pulled on her eyebrows, causing them to arch almost comically, giving her the look of a demented cartoon witch.

Kelly felt instantly ashamed for thinking such bad thoughts about a woman she didn't even know. After all, if Ariel really was interested in Roger, she deserved nothing but Kelly's sympathy.

"Go ahead and get started," Roger said, dismissing her with a wave of his hand. "I'll be along shortly."

He watched her stomp away, then turned back to Kelly. "Kelly, what I'm trying to say is that I think you and I could really be—"

"There you are," Brandon said pleasantly as he strolled up from the opposite direction. "Morning, Hempstead. Hope you slept well."

Roger didn't take his eyes off Kelly as he said, "I plan to sleep even better tonight."

"Good luck with that," Brandon said, and gave him a fraternal slap on the back. "I recommend a cold beer right before bed. Works wonders. Come on, Kelly, weren't you headed over to the concierge desk?"

With that, he maneuvered himself between Kelly and Roger and extracted her arm from the other man's grip. "See you around, Hempstead."

"Are you insane?" she whispered when they were a discreet distance away.

"Did you hear what he said?" Brandon griped. "The guy's delusional. He's got it in his head that you're going to wind up in his bed tonight."

"Yes, I know. And I don't mind letting him think it will happen."

He stopped and glared at her. "Why?"

"Because it'll feel so good to tell him no," she said, her eyes narrowed with rock-solid purpose.

"No?" he repeated.

She glowered at him. "Do you honestly think I would sleep with that man?"

"No," he said slowly, as though it were just occurring to him. "But he doesn't know that."

"Right, and we'll just keep it that way, won't we?"

Brandon frowned in puzzlement, but Kelly merely smiled and said, "Let's please not talk about Roger anymore. I need to get these invoices delivered."

The following night, Brandon wondered for the hundredth time why he hadn't punched Roger in the face when he'd first met him.

Brandon's lead bartender in the wine bar had called in sick, so one of the restaurant waiters was filling in. The hotel was filled to capacity and Brandon was concerned that everything should continue running smoothly. He'd decided to oversee things in the bar until they closed at ten o'clock. If anyone wanted to continue socializing, the restaurant bar would stay open until midnight.

Naturally, Roger the Jerk had chosen this night to tie one on. It was more than clear that the man was a pompous ass who couldn't hold his liquor, but because he was the boss, there was no one around to tell him no, to call it a night and drag him off to his room. If that wasn't bad enough, the more Roger drank, the more impressed with himself he became. At this point, he must've thought he was a regular Fred Astaire, because he'd just grabbed hold of Sherry, the cocktail waitress, and spun her around. Sherry, a consummate professional, had barely managed to keep her tray of drinks from upending.

Personally, Brandon would've loved to have seen Sherry empty all those drinks onto Roger's head, but Brandon knew that wouldn't be good for business. So, with great reluctance, he stepped between them, grabbed hold of Roger's shoulders and turned him in the other direction. "You've had enough, pal."

"You again," Roger slurred. "Back off, will ya? She wants me."

"I'm sure she does," Brandon said, easing his arm around Roger and walking him in the opposite direction. "But I'm doing this for your own good. She's got a wicked right hook, along with a husband who has no sense of humor. He's a big, mean guy. You don't want to piss him off."

"But I can tell she likes me. And she's hot."

"Yeah, pal, I'm sure they all like you," Brandon muttered, leading him toward the door. "Come on, time to call it a night."

The ice queen suddenly appeared at Roger's other side and slipped her arm around his back. "I can take care of him from here."

"Hey, you," Roger exclaimed, pointing a wobbly finger at her. "I know you."

She patted his chest. "Yes, and I know you, too."

"You sure you're okay here?" Brandon asked, concerned that Roger could overpower this thin woman with one careless swipe of his arm.

"Been here, done that," she said, with a brief nod of her head. "I've got it covered."

Roger threw his arm around her shoulders and stared into her face. "How 'bout you and me go back to my room? I've got a hot tub."

"Sounds irresistible," she said, and walked away with him.

Brandon watched them stumble out the door and shook his head in disgust. The man was truly a jackass, but the woman with him seemed okay with that. Guess it took all types. And watching Roger's antics here in the bar tonight, Brandon had clearly recognized Roger's type. He'd seen it before and he didn't like it.

Roger was the type of man who thought he could do whatever he wanted, with whomever he chose, anytime at all. He could drink to excess and order people around with impunity, simply because he had wealth and power. He'd been born with it, grown up knowing it, and now he wielded it like a club.

Brandon had been around plenty of other men like that when he worked in the NFL. Big men who'd always gotten what they wanted by virtue of their size and salary.

Brandon's father had been like that, too, minus the wealth. He'd been a big hulk of a man and he'd used his strength to make others cower. It had been like a game to him, and Brandon and his mother had been his favorite objects of contempt. He'd shown it with his fists.

His father and guys like Roger had a lot in common. Brandon could just imagine what kind of damage a man like that could inflict on someone as gentle and sweet as Kelly. And it made his fists clench and his jaw tighten to know that Kelly had made a date to have dinner with Roger tomorrow night.

Brandon also knew that she'd been putting Roger off

for the last few days, that had the effect of making the guy want her more than ever. The reason Brandon knew this was because he'd been watching her every move. And when Brandon couldn't be around, he'd had others watch her and report back to him. He didn't like Roger, but more than that, he didn't trust him as far as he could kick him.

And while he'd promised Kelly not to do anything that would interfere with her dinner plans with her ex-boyfriend, Brandon had no intention of leaving her truly alone with the guy for a minute. He would remain close by, waiting, watching, making sure that nothing Roger did could ever hurt Kelly again.

The next evening was Kelly's big night. She dressed for her dinner with Roger in a seductive black dress she'd been saving for the occasion. It fit her like a soft, silky glove, with subtle ruching along the sides that accentuated her best curves. Before her makeover, she hadn't even known what ruching was. But now she knew its power, and she liked it. The sleeves of the dress were barely there and the neckline dipped into a heart-shaped curve, nicely showing off just the right amount of cleavage.

She stared at herself in the mirror as she fastened her faux diamond necklace and matching earrings, pleased by her reflection. She'd come a long way and every step had been worth it.

She had decided to join Roger in his elegant suite instead of having dinner in the hotel restaurant. That way, their discussion would be private. In other words, Brandon wouldn't be able to overhear everything and interrupt them for no good reason.

Even though Kelly had known Roger for years and felt perfectly safe with him, she'd gone ahead and checked with the kitchen, just to make sure he had actually ordered dinner. She didn't want him to think he could simply invite her to his room and try to seduce her on an empty stomach. It was a big relief to find out that Roger had, in fact, ordered a lovely dinner for the two of them.

They were to start the evening off with a nice bottle of champagne and a small platter of hors d'oeuvres, then proceed to the entrée of prime rib for two, with chocolate soufflés for dessert. Kelly approved, especially because back when they were dating, Roger had begun to show a touch of cheapness when they dined out. But tonight, he'd pulled out all the stops. Kelly figured he wanted to impress her, and that was exactly what she'd been hoping for.

Now, if she could only get him to beg her to come back to him, her plan would be a success. She would gently refuse him, of course. And if he asked why, she would tell him. He would probably protest and he might even be reduced to insulting her. He excelled at that. But she didn't care. She just wanted the satisfaction of knowing he still found her attractive and wanted her back. Then she could walk out of his life forever and straight into a rosy future.

She had gone over the plan in her mind and even though a part of her knew the whole thing was somewhat petty, she also knew it was something she needed to carry through to the end. Closure. That was her goal. That was all she wanted tonight.

And maybe it was a tiny bit selfish, but she'd been much too nervous to eat lunch earlier, so if she could just arrange to walk out on him *after* she finished that delectable chocolate soufflé, the evening would be a total success.

She never should've come for dinner. The past three hours were a wasted chunk of time she could never get back.

The good news was, the prime rib was cooked to perfection

and the chocolate soufflé was divine. The bad news was, it all sat in her stomach like a brick.

Roger had greeted her at his door looking handsome and debonair in his Armani jacket with his Brooks Brothers pinstriped shirt collar standing up jauntily. She thought the gold ascot was a bit much, but she had to confess that he'd been a perfect gentleman all evening. He'd complimented her and asked her all about life in California. They chatted about mutual friends back East and he shared confidences with her about the people who worked for him.

She was bored stiff.

They'd sipped champagne, nibbled on appetizers, then enjoyed dinner and dessert. And he hadn't made a move on her. What was wrong with him? There simply *must* be something wrong with him tonight. After all, since he'd first checked into the hotel on Monday, he'd been approaching her, seeking her out at least twice a day with an urgency she'd obviously mistaken for desire. Because tonight, there was nothing coming from him. No attraction, no interest, just politeness. A regular snooze-fest.

Maybe it was just as well. After all, she was well and truly *over* Roger. She knew that now. Finally and completely over him. And she had Brandon to thank for it.

"It was such fun catching up with you, Roger," she said, pushing back from the table and standing. "Dinner was wonderful, but I should be going now."

"Kelly, wait," he said, jumping up abruptly and grabbing hold of her hand. "Don't go. We need to talk. About us."

Taken aback, she glanced down at his hand on hers, then up at him. "We've been talking all night, Roger."

He tightened his grip and moved closer. "I know, I know, but I've been holding off saying what needed to be said. Look, Kelly, I want to apologize."

"You do?"

"Yes. God, you look great." He ran his fingers across her shoulder. She shivered, but not in a good way.

"What's this all about, Roger?"

He gritted his teeth, then frowned. He looked vaguely embarrassed. "I've been trying all night to…well, look, I know I said some things I shouldn't have said back when we were together. I was wrong. I was…stupid. But seeing you this week and remembering what we had together, I miss that. I miss you. I want another chance with you. Come back to me, Kelly."

Kelly just stared at him. Now that he was finally saying everything she'd hoped he would say, she didn't believe a single word of it. "I…Roger, I don't know what to say."

"Say yes. Pack your bags and come home with me."

"Roger, I…"

"Wait, don't say a word yet. Just…feel." He made his move, bending his head to kiss her. Actually, it was more of a smashing of his lips against hers.

Maybe it was wrong, but she let him do it. Then he kissed her again with slightly more finesse and Kelly tried really hard to work up some sort of yearning, something, anything. But there was nothing. And she realized it had always been that way. She'd never felt the slightest attraction to Roger. But she'd always thought it was her problem, not his.

Where were the lightning flashes? Where were the fireworks? The rainbows? Sunbursts? She always felt them when Brandon kissed her.

Roger pulled her close and kissed her neck. "Oh, Kelly, we were so good together."

She frowned at that. "We were?"

"You remember." He breathed in her ear. "Don't you feel it all over again when we touch?"

She leaned away to avoid his heavy breath. "I really don't. I'm sorry, Roger. I don't feel anything."

He grabbed her close again. "Yes, you do. I can tell."

"Roger, please don't."

"Now you're just being difficult," he said, trying to angle his head to kiss her again as she tried to push away from him. "Fine, I suppose I deserve some of this after saying the things I said to you five years ago. But you've had your fun. Just admit that you want to come back, and we'll put the past behind us."

With that, he pressed his mouth against hers again and her stomach roiled in protest. She smacked his arm hard enough that he broke off the kiss, giving her a chance to back away from him.

"Don't touch me again," she said when he started walking toward her. "I told you I don't feel the same way about you anymore. I'm leaving now."

He continued to approach her stealthily. "Come on now, Kelly. You're not going to leave after I've spent over three hundred dollars on dinner, are you? You're just nervous because you still don't know how to make love to a man. But don't worry. This time, I'll teach you."

She held up her hand to stop him. "Oh no, you won't. You're the one who doesn't know what you're doing. I know what a really good kiss feels like, Roger. And I just don't feel it from you."

As she stopped to snatch her clutch off the sideboard, Roger grabbed her again. Just then there was a sudden pounding on the door.

Kelly jumped. "What in the world?"

Roger swore loudly. "What is wrong with this damn place?"

"There's nothing wrong with this place!" Kelly said, more insulted by his affront to the hotel than by his disgusting kisses. "There must be something wrong. An emergency."

Someone shouted, "Open up, Hempstead!"

Her eyes widened in shock and she ran to open the door. "Brandon?"

"Duke?" Roger said, scowling at him. "What the hell do you want?"

Brandon walked in and pulled Kelly into his arms. "Are you all right, sweetheart?"

"Take your hands off her, Duke," Roger said in a threatening tone.

"I don't think so," Brandon said, holding her closer.

She took a brief moment to absorb his presence, his scent, his warmth. Then she eased back and gazed up at him. "Brandon, what are you doing here?"

He held Kelly at arm's length and looked her in the eyes. "I know you wanted to get him back, babe. But trust me, he's not the man for you."

Kelly stared at him in bewilderment. "Don't you think I know that?"

"Wait," Roger said. "You want to get me back? Then why aren't you—"

"No," she said immediately, turning to face him. "I didn't want to *get you back*. I wanted to *get back at you*. Big difference."

"I'll say," Brandon said, as his gaze flipped back and forth from Kelly to Roger.

Roger shook his head. "I'm confused."

"Let's get out of here, Kelly," Brandon said, slipping his arm through hers.

"Wait a minute," Roger demanded. "You're leaving with him?"

"Yes, I am."

He snorted. "You think this guy wants you? You really are a fool."

"That's enough, Hempstead," Brandon said quietly.

"Oh, wait. I get it." Roger's laugh was scornful. "You think you're in love with him, don't you? What a load of crap. He just wants you for sex, Kelly. Though God knows why. I'm sure you're still just as lousy in bed as you ever were."

She cringed, but ignored him and kept walking. But Brandon wasn't about to let that go. He turned and said with deceptive calm, "Don't make me hurt you, Hempstead."

But Roger persisted, his eyes wild and desperate. "You can't seriously believe he actually wants you, Kelly. He dates the most beautiful women in the world. Do you really think you can compete with that? You're nothing to him."

She gripped Brandon's arm and forced him to keep walking.

"I mean it, Kelly," Roger said loudly. "You know you'd be better off with me."

At that, Kelly whirled around and shook her finger at him. "No, I wouldn't. I don't mean to be unkind, but you just don't do it for me, Roger. I feel nothing when you kiss me. No spark. No excitement. Nothing. And you know what? It's not my fault. You just don't know how to kiss a woman."

"Fine! Who needs you? Just go," he shouted. As soon as they were out the door, he slammed it behind them.

The night air was crisp and cool as they walked along the wide brick path in silence.

"Well, that was unpleasant," she said finally.

Brandon stopped and studied her in the moonlight. "Are you okay? Did he hurt you?"

"His words were hurtful, but they're nothing I haven't heard before."

He wrapped his arm around her shoulder and pulled her closer. "You managed to get in a few digs."

She nodded. "But it wasn't as satisfying as I thought it would be."

"I'm sorry, sweetheart," Brandon said, as he leaned in close and touched his forehead to hers. "But he's not worth losing sleep over. Especially since he was totally wrong about everything."

"What do you mean?"

"You're fantastic in bed."

She laughed. "You're right."

As they continued walking, she slipped her arm around his waist. "Well, dinner was great anyway. Jean Pierre came through with flying colors."

He chuckled. "Glad to hear it."

After a few more moments, Kelly said, "Roger was right about one thing."

Brandon frowned at her. "No, he wasn't."

"Yes, he was," she said solemnly, and looked up at him. "You only want me for sex."

"You say that like it's a bad thing."

She laughed lightly.

"Come on," he said, squeezing her closer. "Let's go home."

Brandon knew he should've put her to bed and then left her alone. She'd been through a lot with Roger and he could still see remnants of the pain the guy had caused her. But the last thing he wanted to do was leave her with the slightest worry in her mind that anything that schmuck had said was correct.

Tonight, he simply wanted her to feel cherished. Instead of her room, he led her over to his spacious master suite. Once they were inside and the door was closed and locked, he lifted her into his arms and carried her into the bedroom, then eased her down until she was standing beside the bed.

"You look beautiful tonight," he said.

"Thank you," she whispered, gazing up at him.

"Sexy dress." He reached behind her back, found the zipper and maneuvered it down slowly. "But your skin is even sexier."

He slipped her sleeves off and inched the dress down her body, first revealing her luscious full breasts.

"Beautiful." He bent and took first one nipple, then the other into his mouth, licking, nibbling, sucking until she was moaning with delight and Brandon felt her fingers thread through his hair, holding him in place.

Minutes later, he continued removing her dress, baring her skin inch by soft, gorgeous inch until it dropped to the floor. He held her hand as she stepped out of the dress, leaving her wearing a tiny scrap of red lace and her black heels.

"I can never get enough of you in this wardrobe combination," he said, moving his hands over her skin, then dipping his finger between the elastic band of her panties.

"Brandon…"

"I want to feel you surrender."

She hummed with pleasure. "Yes, please."

In one swift move, he tugged the lace free. Then he touched her heat and felt her body arch into his.

Unable to resist, he took two seconds to rip his own shirt off so he could feel her skin against his, then returned his full attention to her hot, wet core.

As he listened to her sighs and whispers of encouragement, he felt his own body harden and burn with the anticipation of filling her completely. He moved to cover her mouth with his, parting her lips with his tongue and sliding inside to taste her essence.

As her breathy groans grew more frantic, his own body tightened with unbearable need. Then she screamed and collapsed against him. He quickly gathered her in his arms and placed her onto the bed. He stripped completely and joined her, wondering if he might expire from the agony of need that had built up inside him.

Blood roared in his ears and he felt himself tremble as he angled his hips and filled her to the hilt. She gasped and lifted herself to allow him to fill her even more, then wrapped her legs around him. They moved in harmony, as though they'd been lovers for years and not just a couple of weeks. He lost himself inside her, lost control, lost sense of everything except the exquisite joining of their bodies as their heartbeats thundered in unison.

He opened his eyes and looked directly into hers and saw the raw desire reflected back at him. As he plunged and thrust to meet her need with his own, he watched as her mouth rounded and she whispered sweet moans of pleasure. The craving for her was so strong, he couldn't resist the pull and he kissed her, swallowing her cries of joy as he followed her to the peak and emptied himself inside her.

Nine

Roger and his group checked out the next day, and Kelly couldn't have been happier or more relieved to see the last of him. As she strolled back to the office along the pretty, flower-lined path, she thought about the night before. Brandon had been right; Roger really was a jackass and seeing him again made her wonder what she'd ever seen in him in the first place. But that didn't matter anymore.

The only thing that mattered was that before he started insulting her last night, Roger had made it clear that he wanted her back in his life. And Kelly had turned him down flat. Everything had gone according to plan. She had to admit it had been painful to see his true colors, but she finally had closure and that felt really good.

But now she had a much bigger problem to deal with. Brandon. She knew she had to be strong and end things with him, for good. They couldn't continue sleeping together, because even though she'd been teasing him the night before, what she'd said was true. He really did only want her for sex!

Well, of course he also wanted to keep her as his office assistant. He'd told her over and over that she was indispensible to their business. That was nice to hear, and she certainly didn't want to lose that part of her life.

But as far as playing the role of his girlfriend? She couldn't do it anymore.

Facts were facts. Brandon never stayed with one woman longer than a month or so, and he'd already spent almost two weeks with Kelly. Two wonderful weeks. She'd much rather have the happy memories contained in those two weeks than suffer through a painful breakup and be left with nothing but sad memories. And no job.

But above and beyond all of those worries, there was one more thorny issue that Kelly hadn't been willing to face until now.

She was in love with Brandon Duke.

"Oh God," she whispered, and sucked in a breath. How foolish could she get?

She'd finally realized it last night when Brandon came rushing into Roger's room to defend her. He'd been her shining knight, willing to break down doors to protect her, and she'd just about melted at the sight of him. That's when it had dawned on her that she'd lost her heart.

So that was it. She was a fool. She'd broken all the rules and fallen in love.

She would never be able to tell Brandon the truth because she knew it would make him uncomfortable. And if he was uncomfortable, it meant that ultimately, she would have to leave her job and then she would never see him again. So she had already decided to say nothing, to brave it out. She would break up with him, and then get back to doing the job he was paying her to do.

It would have to be strictly business between them from now on. And somehow, some way, she would eventually figure out how to get Brandon Duke out of her heart.

Kelly turned on to the highway and headed south.

Instead of facing Brandon with the truth, Kelly had returned to the office, taken one look at her handsome boss and completely chickened out. She'd claimed exhaustion and begged to take the rest of Friday and all day Monday off. Brandon was gracious enough to give her the time, surmising that she had to be wiped out from her unpleasant run-in with Roger.

She hated lying to Brandon, but she wasn't ready to face the truth and do what she had to do. Now she would use the long weekend to gather her thoughts and figure out the best way to deal with her new reality.

She'd packed a small bag and chosen to drive down the coast and home, to Dunsmuir Bay. Less than four hours later, she pulled her car into the driveway of her marina duplex apartment and turned off the engine. Climbing out of the car, she stretched her limbs and breathed deeply, filling her senses with the pungent scent of cool, salty ocean air. It was good to be home.

She spent what was left of the afternoon dusting the living room and bedroom. Then she poured herself a glass of wine and sat on her terrace, trying to think of nothing at all as she stared at the dark blue water and the movement of boats in the marina.

The next morning, she woke up early and went for a long walk along the waterfront. On her way back, she detoured through the charming block-long section of shops and restaurants known as Old Town Dunsmuir. The intoxicating scent of baked goods lured her into CUPCAKE, Julia Duke's bakery.

She was cheered by the bright blue and white décor and attractive bistro-style tables and chairs that lined the wide, bay windows on either side of the door. She stepped up to the counter and began to drool over the view of so many delicate pastries stacked neatly inside the case.

"Kelly?" someone said.

She glanced over at a small table at the opposite end of the room and saw Julia, Trish and Sally Duke sitting together, enjoying lattes and freshly baked scones.

"Come join us," Sally said.

"Oh, I don't want to intrude on your breakfast."

"You're kidding, right?" Julia teased, and pulled a chair over from a nearby table. "Come sit down. What are you doing here?"

She sat down and smiled gratefully. "I decided to take a few days off and drive down to open up my apartment. We'll be moving back to headquarters in another week or so and I wanted to be prepared."

"Oh, I'll be so glad to have you both back in town," Sally said.

"I'll be glad, too."

Julia stood. "Let me get you a latte."

"Oh, please don't go to any trouble."

"It's no trouble, it's my job," she said with a grin. Just then, Lynnie, the counter girl, came over to take her order and refill Trish's teacup, so Julia sat down again.

"It was great to see you all up in Napa," Kelly said.

"We had a wonderful time," Trish said. "I still dream about Ingrid's magical massages and wake up moaning. I'm sure Adam's getting all sorts of strange ideas."

They all laughed.

"Your husbands are both so wonderful," Kelly said to Trish and Julia. "I probably shouldn't say anything because they're my bosses, after all, but it's so nice to see how much in love they are with both of you."

"It's lovely, isn't it?" Sally said, smiling fondly at her daughters-in-law. "But what about you, Kelly? Wasn't this the week you were going to see a special visitor from your past?"

"Sounds intriguing," Julia said, pulling her chair closer. "Tell us everything."

Kelly laughed. "Oh, it all amounted to a bunch of nothing, really."

"But that's why you wanted the makeover, wasn't it?"

"Yes." Kelly felt herself blush and was glad that Lynnie brought her latte just then. She took a few sips to hide the awkwardness she felt.

"Oh, come on, don't stop now, tell us what happened," Trish said.

Julia patted Kelly's hand. "We promise it won't leave this room, if you're worried that Brandon will find out."

"I'm not worried about that," Kelly said with a frown. "He was right in the middle of it."

"Curiouser and curiouser," Julia said.

They all laughed again, and Kelly went ahead and spilled the story of Roger breaking up with her years ago and her wanting to get back at him.

"He sounds vile," Julia said.

"I'm just happy you got to eat a full dinner," Trish said, rubbing her stomach as the Duke women commiserated with her.

Kelly laughed again. "Yeah, I was happy about that, too." She took another sip of her latte, glad that she'd decided to stop by the bakery. She really liked these women and felt a bond with them, even though she didn't really fit in. Yes, she was sleeping with one of the Duke men, too. But they didn't know about that. And it was over anyway.

That thought was too depressing, so she swept it out of her mind for now.

"This back pain is getting worse," Trish said, arching and twisting to find a more comfortable position. "I hope it doesn't last much longer."

"How long has it been bothering you?" Sally asked.

"All morning."

"Any contractions?"

"Yes, but they don't mean anything. I'm not due for three more days."

Sally and Julia exchanged looks.

"Should we call Adam?" Kelly asked.

"No, no," Trish said, her voice sounding a bit weaker as she stretched her shoulders. "He's at the office today. They've got another big closing this week. I guess you all know that."

"I'll drive you home," Sally offered.

"Or to the hospital," Kelly said.

Trish waved them away. "I'm fine. It'll pass. I'd much rather hear more dirt on Roger. It'll distract me from my aches and pains."

Sally's smile was strained. "Yes, Kelly, and tell us how in the world Brandon got in the middle of this mess."

Kelly willingly explained what happened when Brandon pounded on the door and everyone was impressed by his heroics.

"Uh-oh," Trish said, trying to stand up. "I hate to interrupt the story, but I think my water just broke."

"Don't move," Kelly said, and helped Trish ease back down in the chair. Kelly grabbed her phone and called the office to alert Adam, telling him to meet Trish at the hospital and offering to alert his brothers. That wasn't necessary, since Adam was on a conference call with both men at that moment.

Julia ran into the kitchen and brought back clean dish-cloths.

Sally rubbed Trish's back. "Oh, honey, I'm sorry you're in pain, but I'm so excited. We're going to have a baby!"

At the hospital, Kelly kept trying to leave but Sally wouldn't let her.

"But I'm not part of the family," she protested.

"Yes, you are," Sally insisted. "Besides, you're so cool and calm under pressure, much better than any of us. So if you don't mind, I'd appreciate it if you'd stay."

"Okay, maybe for a little while."

Adam came racing down the hall. "Where is she?"

"She's right inside that room," Sally said, and grabbed Adam's arm. "Take a deep breath first and relax. And fix your hair or you're likely to scare her to death."

"Right." Adam sucked in some air and let it out. His hair looked like he'd been grabbing it to keep from going crazy on the drive from his office to the hospital, so now he smoothed it back with his fingers. Then he grabbed Sally and planted a big kiss on her cheek. "I love you, Mom."

Kelly smiled as happy tears sprang to Sally's eyes.

Cameron jogged down the hall a moment later and greeted Julia with a kiss, then turned to Sally and Kelly. "Brandon's taking the jet down so he should be here in an hour or so."

"Good," Sally said after pulling Cameron close for a hug. "I know Adam will want you all to be here."

Hearing that Brandon would be arriving soon, Kelly touched Sally's arm. "I really should go."

"Please don't," Sally said, then paused and took a long

look at Kelly. "Sweetie, did you want to leave because Brandon is coming?"

"No," she said too quickly, causing Sally's eyebrows to arch.

"Let's have a seat over here," Sally suggested. "I want to ask you something."

Kelly didn't dare refuse or Sally would be even more suspicious, so she followed the older woman over to a quiet corner seating arrangement.

"Now Kelly," Sally began, "I don't mean to pry, but I'm concerned. Do you have feelings for Brandon?"

"Well, of course," she said, trying for a casual tone. "We've worked together for years and he's a great guy. I like him."

Sally folded her arms across her chest. "I think you know what I mean."

Kelly couldn't exactly lie to Brandon's mother so she came clean. "Yes, I know what you mean, and yes, I do like Brandon. A lot. But I also know him really well, and I know that a relationship between us would never work out. He's got women lined up from here all the way to New York City, Mrs. Duke."

"Yes, I know."

"Gorgeous, sophisticated women," she continued with a note of resignation she couldn't disguise. "I can't deal with that kind of competition."

"Oh, I think you can," Sally said.

Kelly shook her head and tried to smile. "Thank you, but I really can't. And even if I could, Brandon just isn't a one-woman man. He goes through them like...well..." She stopped and frowned. It wouldn't be polite to give Sally too many details about her son and all the women in his life.

"Oh, don't bother trying to sugarcoat it, sweetie," Sally

said with a shake of her head. "I know my sons have always been popular with women."

"To say the least," Kelly muttered.

Sally took hold of her hand. "I also know that Brandon is a good, good man, and he's so worthy of love."

"I think so, too," Kelly whispered. "I really do. I just wish, well, I wish I was the one he wanted."

Sally hugged her. "If it means anything at all, I would love it if you were."

Kelly felt tears spring to the surface and she brushed them away. "That's so sweet of you. Thank you."

Sally's eyes narrowed in steely resolve and she murmured something Kelly wasn't sure she heard correctly. But it sounded something like, "We'll just see how sweet I can be."

Brandon walked swiftly down the hospital hall and into the large waiting room. Glancing around, he spied his mother sitting with Julia and Cameron. His brother held a sleepy little Jake against his shoulder.

"What's going on?" Brandon asked.

"Oh sweetie, I'm so glad you're here." Sally jumped up and gave him a hug, then walked with him out into the hall.

Brandon took another visual sweep of the room but didn't see Kelly anywhere. Adam had said that she was the one who had called him earlier to say that Trish was going into labor. So for the last two hours, Brandon had been wondering what the hell Kelly was doing back in Dunsmuir Bay. He'd tried calling her when the plane landed, but she wasn't answering her cell phone. And that rarely happened.

He'd known she was upset about Roger, but now he was

worried that there might be something else bothering her. Otherwise, she would've answered her cell phone.

He glanced up and down the hall. Maybe she'd just gone off to the ladies' room for a minute.

"Are you looking for someone?" his mother asked.

"Yeah, I thought Kelly would be here. Adam said she was on her way to the hospital with all of you."

"She was here for a while, but she left."

"Oh. Is she coming back?"

"I don't know," Sally said, looking a little puzzled. "She seemed to be concerned about not being here when you showed up."

"Not being here?" Now it was Brandon's turn to be puzzled. "Why wouldn't she want to be here when I got here?"

"She said that she wasn't part of the family, so she thought it best if she left."

"What?" he said in disbelief, then muttered, "Well, that's dumb."

"Is it?" she asked.

"Okay, Mom, what are you getting at?"

"We talked about this before, Brandon," she said. "I thought we were in agreement. But now I have to ask you, are you involved with Kelly?"

"Why? What did she say?"

Sally rolled her eyes. "She didn't say a word, but she seemed uncomfortable sticking around. And you didn't answer the question."

"Come on, Mom, let it go."

But his mother gave him "the look," and he capitulated.

"Okay, fine, but it's not like we're really involved. We're just having a good time."

"Oh, sweetie." Sally shook her head. "I don't think Kelly is that kind of girl."

"You've said that before," he said, rubbing his jaw in frustration. "I'm not even sure I know what you mean."

"Yes, you do. She's not as sophisticated as most of the women you date. She doesn't know the rules of the game like those women do. Kelly's sensitive and sweet. She wants to meet a nice guy and fall in love and settle down. And we both know that's not you."

"Hey, I'm a nice guy."

She patted his arm. "Yes, you are, and I know you wouldn't hurt her deliberately. But if you don't stop seeing her, you're going to break her heart."

Trish gave birth to an eight-pound baby boy at two o'clock the following morning. They named the baby Tyler Jackson Duke. Despite the late hour, Adam passed out cigars to his brothers and the whole family celebrated with champagne and apple juice for Trish. Brandon snapped a picture with his phone and sent it along with a text message to Kelly, announcing the birth. A few hours later, he received a two-word message back from her. "Congratulations, Uncle!"

So at least she was communicating with him again, Brandon thought with relief. He decided not to press her any further, knowing he would see her on Tuesday, less than two days from now. By then, she would be long over Roger and back to being her old self. Then she and Brandon could talk about a few things. Meanwhile, as long as he was in Dunsmuir Bay, he'd planned a busy day for himself that centered on finding new and creative ways to spoil his brand-new bouncing baby nephew.

Ten

Tuesday morning, Brandon walked across the wide terrace toward his office, amused to find he had a spring in his step. He knew where it had come from.

Kelly would be back in the office today and he was really looking forward to seeing her again.

But when he walked into the office, she wasn't at her desk, and he felt a trickle of panic seep down his spine. He ruthlessly shoved the feeling away. It was no big deal. In fact, it was still early. She would be here any minute.

He walked into his inner office, took off his jacket and hung it on the back of his door. Sitting at his desk, he pulled up his calendar to study what was in store for the week. Meetings, conference calls and the start of organizing the move back to headquarters in Dunsmuir Bay. The brief visit home over the weekend had reminded him just how much he missed his family and all the amazing advantages there were to living on the California coast.

It was a full ten minutes later when he finally heard Kelly walk in. A part of him he hadn't even realized was tense began to relax.

"Morning, Kelly," he called. "Come on in when you're settled."

"Okay."

A few minutes later, after starting the coffee and powering up her computer, she walked in.

Brandon looked up and started to grin, then felt his mouth drop open. She was dressed in an old, dull gray pantsuit with a black turtleneck underneath. Her hair was pulled back in a ponytail and she wore the thick horned-rim glasses he thought she'd destroyed.

"What happened to you?" he asked before he could stop himself, then quickly shook his head. "I mean, did you lose your contact lenses?"

"No, the glasses are just easier," she explained. "Now that Roger's gone, I thought I'd go back to wearing some of my more comfortable outfits. This looks okay, doesn't it?"

"Yeah, sure," he said, stymied by her decision.

"Good." She hesitated, then sat down in the chair in front of his desk. "We need to talk, Brandon."

"Okay, let's talk," he said, and watched her take her glasses off and fiddle with them nervously.

Studying her, he realized she looked even better than ever, without any makeup on. True, those pants she wore were too damned baggy and the color did nothing to complement her complexion, but Brandon knew that underneath all that material was a stunning pair of world-class legs. The sudden image of her naked thighs caused his groin to stiffen instantly. With a silent groan, he wheeled his chair closer to his desk to mask the problem.

She took a deep breath and finally started talking. "Don't be angry, but I have to thank you."

He scowled at her. "I thought we'd agreed you wouldn't do that."

"I'm sorry, but I can't help it," she said. "Just let me get through this, okay?"

"Of course. Go ahead."

"Okay." After another deep breath, she said, "First, I have to thank you for helping me prepare for Roger's visit. I think you know what I mean by that. And second, thank you for coming to his hotel room door when you did. Your timing was perfect and it was nice to know that you had my back while I was in there sparring with Roger."

He grinned. "Right. You're welcome."

"Good," she said with a nod of her head. "I'm happy to say that I've kept my original bargain not to fall for you, and now I'm ready to go back to life as we knew it before my ex-boyfriend's name was ever mentioned in this office."

"And what does that mean, exactly, Kelly?"

She refused to meet his gaze as she clutched her hands together in her lap. "It means, you know, we'll no longer be sleeping together."

"Sleeping together."

"Oh, you know." She looked up and her smile was shaky. "Not that I didn't enjoy every moment, I really did. You know I did. But…I'm sorry, Brandon, it's time to end things, once and for all. It was wonderful, but I'm…so sorry." With that, she bolted out of the chair and walked briskly out of his office, closing the door behind her.

As he watched her go, he pondered her words. Part of him was highly dissatisfied with her decision not to continue with their sexual arrangement.

On second thought, *all* of him was dissatisfied. Hell, he

wanted her right now. Even in that ugly suit of hers, she was hotter than any woman he'd known in a long time.

Leaning his elbows on the desk, he thought about his next move. Maybe he would let her stew for a few hours, then ask her to have dinner with him tonight. A great meal, a few glasses of wine, and he was confident they'd end up back in his bed again.

His mother's words suddenly echoed in his brain. Damn, that was the problem with having a conscience. He knew Sally was right. Kelly was sweet and sensitive and deserved to find love some day. If Brandon had his way and their affair continued, Kelly would wind up being hurt eventually. If he wasn't careful, he might just break her heart.

But what about Brandon's heart?

He sat back in his chair and rubbed his chest thoughtfully. Maybe he'd pulled a muscle because for some strange reason, he felt an aching twinge that felt almost like grief.

Brandon asked her out to dinner that night and she politely refused.

The next day, he asked her to join him for lunch and she said she had other plans.

Finally, he asked her if she'd like to come to his room later that evening.

"You know I can't do that, Brandon," she said and tried to smile.

"I figured it was worth a shot," he said.

"I'm sorry," she said, staring up at him from her desk chair. "This whole situation is my fault."

"How's that?"

"It was completely unprofessional of me to drag you into my problems in the first place. But now I'm just anxious for everything to return to business as usual. I hope you can help me do that."

"Right. Okay. Sure." He nodded and walked back into his office, and Kelly had to take great gulping breaths to keep from bursting into tears.

She wasn't sure she could continue working in the same office with him every day. But the alternative was to never see him again and there's no way she could go through that.

She simply had to stop thinking about kissing him and touching him. She had to stop thinking about the way he had touched her and made her laugh. She just had to stop thinking! And she would.

It might take another thirty or forty years, but she was absolutely positive she would get over him.

"It's your mother on line two," Kelly announced over the intercom line.

"Thanks, Kelly," he said, and pressed the button. "Hi, Mom."

"Hi, sweetie, I haven't heard from you all week so I'm calling to make sure you're all right."

"I'm fine. How are you doing?"

"Oh, everything is wonderful. The baby is so beautiful." She went on for five minutes about the joy of baby Tyler. When she finally exhausted that subject, she said, "How's Kelly?"

"She's fine," he said. "Why do you ask?"

"You sound a little irritated. Is everything all right?"

"Sure, why wouldn't it be?" Brandon snapped. "Kelly seems to have forgotten that we ever had sex with each other in the first place, so things are just dandy."

"Ah," she said.

What the hell? Did he really just say that out loud?

Great. Now if only he could kick himself in the ass, everything would be fan-freaking-tastic. "Sorry, Mom, I'm just a little busy right now."

But she wasn't buying that line. "Brandon, are you in love with Kelly?"

"What?" he shouted.

"No need to yell," she said softly. "Sweetie, why else would you be so upset that she doesn't want to sleep with you?"

"Who said I was upset?"

She started laughing, which just annoyed him more.

"Look, Mom, I really don't have time for—"

"Now you listen to me, Brandon Duke. It's as clear as the nose on your face that you're in love with that girl, and I expect you to marry her."

"Mom, what've you been smoking?"

"Very funny, Brandon," she said drily. "You can deny it all you want but I know you better than you know yourself."

He sighed. "I really have to go. I love you, Mom."

"I love you too, son. Call me later and tell me how it went. Bye-bye."

He hung up the phone and rubbed his neck. Damn, between his mother's wild assumptions and Kelly's stiff-shirted business competence, he was likely to go insane.

For the past three days, he'd managed to put up with Kelly's firm need to work professionally and reliably in his office. She was the ultimate assistant, always answering his phones, making his coffee, transcribing his calls, typing his letters, being polite and businesslike at all times.

It was enough to make him spit nails.

He'd made it clear when she returned from Dunsmuir Bay that he would be more than happy to continue their sexual relationship. But Kelly had refused him. He might've asked her again once or twice, maybe three times more during the week. Okay, maybe four times, max.

All of a sudden, she'd turned on him and accused him of being attracted to her only because she'd gotten her makeover!

He'd attempted to deny it, but she'd seen right through him. She'd asked him point-blank, how could she trust his feelings for her now if that was the only reason he'd originally been interested in her?

It seemed an unfair question given his almost constant state of arousal these past few days. Because the irony was, even though she'd gone back to wearing her drab and dowdy pantsuits, he was still getting turned on whenever she walked into the room. But now that he could safely admit that her getting a makeover had nothing to do with his attraction to her, she didn't want to hear him out.

And ever since she'd asked the question, Brandon had seriously wondered why he'd never realized how sexy she was before. Because now it was so damned obvious.

She was a beautiful woman in every way and he couldn't keep his eyes off her whenever she walked into a room. And if he didn't see her right away, he would catch a whiff of her scent, and it drove him wild with desire. But when he accused her of wearing too much perfume, she had the audacity to claim that she never wore perfume.

So maybe he really was going crazy. Maybe he needed a vacation. But where would he go? He already lived in a beautiful part of California and that was pretty close to paradise. He didn't know where to go or what to do and he didn't care. All he knew was that he couldn't keep seeing Kelly every hour of every day and not hold her in his arms again.

"I'll be back in a while," he said to her and rushed out of the office. He headed for his room and once he was there, he decided to go for a run. It would be good to work off some of this insanity. Maybe he'd eaten some bad mushrooms and his brain was filled with toxins. It could happen. Exercise was the answer.

As he ran, he contemplated the situation objectively. He had to admit that breaking up with Kelly had been the best for both of them. She was his employee, after all, and he shouldn't have taken advantage of her in the first place. Of course, that wasn't really fair because, after all, the whole affair had been her idea.

He smiled at the thought, then chuckled. Okay, he was willing to admit that maybe he'd nudged her in the right direction. But nothing changed the fact that it was still best if they didn't sleep together again. But damn, he missed her, and not just in bed. She had a savvy business mind and it was fun to bounce ideas back and forth with her. She made him laugh. How many women had ever made him laugh?

But that didn't matter, because his mother was right about one thing, much as he hated to admit it. Kelly had "white picket fence" practically tattooed across her forehead. She deserved a good man who would love her and treat her right, give her a couple of kids, plus a dog, a couple of hamsters and a fish bowl.

The fact that he hated to picture another man in her bed was something he didn't dwell on too deeply.

Somewhere during his fifth mile, as his breath wheezed out and he had to sweep the sweat from his eyes, Brandon figured out the solution to his problem. It was so simple. He just needed to get laid.

Tonight he would make a few calls to some women he knew, arrange a date or two for the weekend, and participate in some mind-blowing sex. And maybe then this out-of-control desire for Kelly would disappear.

* * *

Kelly adjusted her glasses and continued typing the letter Brandon had dictated. She hated these old eyeglasses but she knew it was better to wear them and look drab, if only to keep Brandon at a distance.

Today, she wore the dark purple pantsuit she'd owned forever. It was so old, it still had lumpy shoulder pads sewn into the jacket. With her sensible brown shoes and her hair pulled back, she looked like someone's maiden aunt. But she could live with that.

It helped to stare at herself in the mirror each morning after she was dressed and ready to go and realize she truly had no business falling in love with her handsome boss. *You are a total cliché,* she would repeat to herself daily. But no matter how many times she had scolded herself, she still hadn't been able to keep from rushing right toward that cliff.

Every time she saw him, she had to fight to ignore her feelings. After all, it wasn't as if he would ever ask her to marry him, for God's sake. So who was she trying to fool? He would never settle down, certainly not with her. A woman would have to be a blithering idiot to think that he would, and Kelly had never been an idiot. Well, not until recently, anyway.

The door swung open and an absolutely beautiful woman walked into the office. She was tall and willowy, with long flowing blond hair and the bluest eyes Kelly had ever seen. Were those contact lenses? No, they had to be real. She was too perfect, too ethereal, not to be completely real.

Kelly shook her head in defeat as she recognized the woman. This was Bianca Stephens, the beautiful wicked witch of her nightmares. Live and in person. And she was the most stunning woman Kelly had ever seen.

"You must be Karen," she said haughtily. "I'm here to see Brandon. He's expecting me."

Kelly didn't have the strength or interest to correct her name again, nor did she care to have the unpleasant woman standing around glaring at her while she checked with Brandon.

"Go right in," Kelly said, and swept her hand toward Brandon's closed door.

"I certainly will."

Bianca closed the door behind her and Kelly felt as though the wind had been knocked out of her. She slumped forward and laid her head on her desk. This was the last straw. She couldn't take it anymore.

When she realized she was crying, she knew she had to act immediately. She couldn't continue living like this. She was hopelessly in love with the big jerk in the next room and she could no longer sit by and watch him play his games with other women.

She was finished making romantic dinner reservations for him and his flavor of the week. She was finished buying diamond tennis bracelets for his civilized breakups.

She was finished.

With all the energy she could muster, she sat up and wiped the tears away, then quickly typed a letter of resignation and emailed it to him. Pulling her purse from the bottom drawer, she stood up and walked out of the office.

"Hello, Brandon darling," Bianca said, closing the door behind her.

"Bianca," he said, unable to disguise his shock.

"Aren't you happy to see me?"

"Uh, yeah, sure," he said, pushing away from his desk and standing to greet her. "But what are you doing here?"

"It was just so good to hear from you the other night," she said, kissing his cheek, then using her little finger to smooth her lipstick. It was a move meant to entice and he'd seen her do it a dozen times before. He watched as she strolled over to the floor-to-ceiling window and gazed nonchalantly at the view. "I didn't feel like waiting for the weekend, so I had Gregory drive me out here to you."

"I see."

She spread her arms in invitation. "And here I am. Are you happy to see me?"

"Happy? Yeah, sure." He looked beyond Bianca over to the closed door. "Did you see my assistant out there?"

"Yes, and honestly, Brandon, I can't believe you still have that rude woman working for you."

"Rude? Kelly?"

"I shouldn't criticize," she said, staring at her fingernails, "but she was very unpleasant to me on the phone the other day."

"Kelly?" Distracted now, Brandon checked his telephone. There was no red light to indicate that his trusted assistant was on the phone. So why hadn't she buzzed him to warn him about Bianca? Where the hell was she? "I'm a little busy today, Bianca."

"Too busy for me?" she said, pouting.

Okay, that might've come across a little harsh. "Uh, no, of course not. It's nice to see you."

"I certainly hope so," she said. "I've come all this way."

He stared at her for a moment. He'd forgotten how beautiful she was, and how self-centered. "Yeah. What a surprise. I just need to handle a few things…"

"You're going to keep working?"

"Just for a minute," he said, folding up the files that were spread on his desk. "Then I guess we can go have a drink or something."

"Sounds yummy." She sat in his visitor's chair and pulled out her smartphone. "I'll just sit here and check my messages until you're ready."

"Fine."

A soft ding came from his computer and he rushed to check his email. It was from Kelly. Good. Maybe she was going to explain exactly how in the hell Bianca had gotten in here.

He opened the message, skimmed the words, but couldn't believe them. *Two weeks' notice...Resignation... Thank you for the opportunity...*

"What?" He stood up. "No, no, no."

"No?" Blanca said.

He stared at her again, wondering why she was here. But he knew why. He was the one who'd called her and told her he wanted to see her. What the hell was wrong with him? He shook his head and muttered, "I'm an idiot."

"Brandon?" Bianca said. "Are you ill?"

He'd made a huge mistake.

"Sorry, Bianca," he said, pulling her gently from the chair and walking her to the door. "You'll have to tell Gregory to drive you back to the city. Something's come up."

He raced out the door.

Kelly had just pulled her suitcase out of the closet when the pounding began. She sighed as she walked across the room to answer the door.

Brandon stood there, looking so handsome, so tall and rugged. And so concerned. "You can't just leave me."

"I'm not just leaving you," she said, leading him into her room. "I'm giving you two weeks' notice."

"But why? Did Bianca say something to make you angry? Is that what this is about?"

"No, of course not." She opened a drawer, grabbed a neatly stacked pile of shirts and put them in her suitcase.

"She did. She said something. I knew it." He paced across the floor. "I've sent her away. I didn't ask her to come to the office, Kelly. She's gone and you'll never see her again. You can't quit."

"Yes, I can. And it's not about Bianca." Kelly shook her head, still a little horrified that Brandon could enjoy spending time with someone as awful as Bianca. But that was none of her business. Not anymore.

"Then why are you leaving? We work really well together."

"We do. Or we did." She smiled sadly at him as she stacked a few pairs of jeans into her suitcase. "But then I broke the rules."

"What rules?" he asked as he walked back and forth behind her. "What are you talking about?"

"The ground rules, remember?" She took a deep breath and turned to gaze up at him. "I fell in love with you, Brandon."

He was stunned into silence.

"I know," she said lightly, reaching for her lingerie and tossing it all onto the bed. "It was a shock to me, too."

"What?" He grabbed her and whipped her around to face him. "No. No, you didn't. I'm a jerk, remember? A big baby when I'm sick. I'm…I'm superstitious. You'd be crazy to fall for me, remember? That's what you said. And you promised you wouldn't…"

"I know what I promised," she said. "And I'm really sorry, but it looks like I wasn't able to keep my word."

"I don't believe it."

"It's true." She patted his arm and stepped back. "I'm sorry."

He blew out a heavy breath, then said slowly, "It had to

be Bianca's fault. When she walked in, you got mad and left."

"I'm not mad," she insisted, shaking her head.

"Then why did you leave? She's gone. I don't want her around. I realized that as soon as I saw her. Was she rude to you? She can be a little abrasive."

"Oh, Brandon." Kelly smiled sadly. "Don't you see? If it's not Bianca, it'll be someone else. My point is, there will always be other women in your life."

"But I want *you* in my life."

"I want you, too, but not in the way you're talking about. Look, I know you're not in love with me. And that's okay. You're not the sort of man to settle down with one woman and I've always known that. This isn't your fault. I'm the one who broke the rules."

"I forgive you."

She laughed. "Thank you. But today I realized that I can't sit outside your office and watch women come and go. Call me a weakling, but I can no longer go shopping for gifts for the women you're sleeping with. I'm sorry."

He grabbed her hands. "This is all my fault."

"How do you figure?" she asked, forcing herself to look into his deep blue eyes.

"We were just too good together. But that's not love, Kelly," he hastened to explain. "That's just good sex."

She laughed again, then realized she'd begun to cry and ruthlessly swiped away the tears. "Yes, the sex was good, really good. But I know my own heart, Brandon. I know that what I feel for you is love, and I know you don't feel the same. I'm okay with that."

"Well, maybe I'm not."

"I'm sorry. But you must understand, I can't work for you anymore."

"Damn, Kelly." He raked his fingers through his hair in frustration. "I don't know what to do to make this right."

"There's nothing you can do to make it right. I'll stay on for two weeks and hire my replacement. Then I'll leave."

The two weeks went by too quickly, and before Brandon was ready to deal with the change, Kelly was gone. Her replacement was Sarah, an older woman so amazingly well organized that she scared Brandon a little. Kelly had trained the woman so well that in no time at all, she could do almost everything as well as her predecessor had.

But she wasn't Kelly.

Sarah organized the major office move back to Dunsmuir Bay, and it went flawlessly from start to finish. Brandon was back in his office without a wrinkle in his schedule. Sarah was an organizational genius.

But she wasn't Kelly.

Brandon knew he would snap out of this funk any day now. After all, it wasn't like he was in love with Kelly. He wasn't in love with anyone. He didn't *do* love. It was just that he missed her. And why not? They'd worked together for over four years. That was all. They'd gotten to know each other well and it was weird that she wasn't around. That was all it was.

And he'd get over it. As usual, he knew exactly what he needed to do to wipe her out of his mind. He would have to make some more phone calls. He had to find another woman to take her place. Not Bianca of course, remembering her visit. Why had he ever wanted to spend time with that vacuous, vain woman? There were plenty of other women out there.

But frankly, he couldn't quite imagine himself having a romantic conversation with another woman. He couldn't picture himself sitting across a dinner table, asking another woman about herself, sharing a bottle of wine, spending an entire evening with her, whoever she might be. He tried to picture the sort of woman he'd dated in the past, tried to remember what he'd talked about with them. But he couldn't remember. They had all faded into the fog and now all he could recall were the fun times with Kelly, when they'd talked and laughed and shared secrets for hours. Whenever he tried to imagine spending time with someone else, he found himself bored to death.

So he buried himself in work, knowing he would snap out of it any day now.

The following Saturday, Adam and Trish invited everyone over to see the baby. Brandon pulled up in front of their sprawling Craftsman home and parked his car, then sat with his hands on the wheel and contemplated whether he should even go inside the house. It had been an effort to get out of bed that morning and he wondered if he'd caught some kind of flu. He didn't want to be around the baby if he was sick.

But his head and sinuses were perfectly clear and he wasn't coughing or anything. His stomach was fine, although he hadn't given a lot of thought to fine dining lately. And he was feeling kind of run-down. He chalked it up to the big move back home and climbed out of the car.

Cameron stood on the front porch. "Hey, did you forget the beer?"

"Nope, got it right here," he said, and jogged back around to the trunk of his car. He shook his head as he grabbed the case of beer he'd bought ten minutes ago on the way over to Adam's house. Where was his brain today?

He found himself asking that same question all afternoon. Whenever his mother or brothers asked him a question, he'd realize halfway through his answer that he'd wandered off on some tangent or another.

They were gathered around the wide bar that separated the kitchen from the family room when his mother finally reached up and pressed the back of her hand to his forehead. "Are you feeling all right, sweetie?"

"Yeah, I'm fine," he said, and grabbed a tortilla chip. "Just a little distracted."

"I hope you're not coming down with something."

"Nope, just working too hard. I might need a vacation."

"Oh, speaking of vacation, I ran into Kelly yesterday," Julia said as she crossed the kitchen with a bowl of salsa. "She just got back from visiting her family. She looks wonderful."

Brandon's ears perked up. "She was back east?"

"That's right," Sally said, dragging a chip through the fresh salsa. "You know her family lives in Vermont."

"Yeah." He studied his beer bottle.

Julia sipped her lemonade. "Roger lives in her hometown, doesn't he?"

"Roger?" Brandon felt the sudden, bitter taste of bile in his throat. "She saw Roger when she went home?"

Trish shut the refrigerator door and turned. "Well, they're both in the same town."

There was no way Kelly had gone back east to see Roger. Brandon knew that in his gut. She wouldn't waste a minute of her time with him. But if Roger was from her hometown, maybe he knew her family. Maybe Kelly's father knew Roger's father. Had her family wanted her to marry Roger? Hell. Brandon knew all about family pressure.

"Sweetie, you do look pale," Sally said, clutching his arm.

Brandon swallowed the last of his beer. "I just need a damn vacation."

He decided to spend a few days back at the Napa resort, but he didn't go there as the boss. Instead, he brought along his oldest boots, his rattiest blue jeans, some tattered shirts, and put himself to work in the vineyards.

As teenagers, Brandon and his brothers had spent a few summers on construction sites around Dunsmuir Bay, so he knew what hard labor was good for. It was basic and tough and real. Sweat and hard work helped a man think about his life, what was authentic and what was fantasy, what was important and what was crap. At the end of a long day, a man could look around and see what he'd accomplished.

As Brandon walked across the fields past the newly weeded and raked rows of grapevines, whose leaves were dry and brittle in the autumn twilight, he looked around and saw what he'd accomplished.

And he knew exactly what was missing.

Kelly had been back from Vermont for over a week now and knew it was time to start compiling her list of social organizations. She'd been putting the task off for long enough. She had a goal, remember? It was time to dive into the dating pool before she grew too old to swim.

There was a knock on her door and Kelly's heart fluttered in her chest.

"Oh, stop it," she scolded herself as she glanced up at the wall clock. It had to be the mailman, that was all. Brandon didn't even know where she lived! What earthly reason would he have for being here? Would she always flip out every time the doorbell chimed or the telephone rang? She put the last dish away in the cabinet and hung up the damp dish towel, then walked over to open the front door.

And forgot how to breathe.

"B-Brandon?"

"Hey, Kelly," he said. "Listen, I need some help."

She blinked, not quite believing her eyes. He stood leaning against her doorjamb looking better than she remembered, and she remembered him looking pretty darn good.

"You gonna let me come in?" he asked.

"Oh, sure." She swung the door open wider for him. "Did Sarah quit?"

"No." He walked into her home, filling the space. "Sarah's fine. She does good work."

"Oh. Okay." She closed the door and stared at him. It had been four long weeks since she'd last seen him and she'd spent all that time trying to stay busy, trying not to think about him, trying to get on with her life. She'd traveled back east for a week to see her father and sisters and their families. It had been a lovely visit, but the trip had cemented in her the understanding that Dunsmuir Bay was truly her home. Now she just had to put the pieces of her life back together. She'd started her list of dating possibilities. And she'd spent all day yesterday on her computer, searching the various employment sites, looking for a new job. She had a list of promising prospects and she planned to send résumés tomorrow.

But now, seeing Brandon, she couldn't remember exactly what any of those job prospects were.

"This is a nice place," he said, glancing around, then walking over to the wide picture window. "Great view."

"Thank you." Was he even taller than she remembered?

Maybe it was seeing him in her house for the first time that made her think so. She licked her lips nervously. "You said you needed my help with something?"

"Yeah." He seemed to consider something for a moment, then walked up close and took hold of her hand. Kelly tried not to focus on the fact that her hand fit so perfectly in his.

He gazed down, then back at her. "You know, this is a little embarrassing. I wonder if maybe we could sit and talk for a few minutes."

"Okay." She led the way to her comfortable sofa and he sat down way too close to her. "What is it, Brandon?"

"The thing is, Kelly, I need some help with my kissing. I'm not sure if I'm doing it right anymore."

She tried to swallow around her suddenly dry throat. "You're kidding, right?"

"Nope. I'm desperate."

She shook her head. "Brandon, you're the last man on earth who needs help with his kissing."

"See, that's where you're wrong," he said, clutching her hand more tightly.

"Okay, fine. But you could get any woman in the world to help you out. Why are you here?"

"Well, that's the thing." He touched her cheek, then ran his fingers through her hair. "I found out it only works right when I'm kissing the person I love."

"Oh Brandon," she said on a sigh.

"I'm in love with you, Kelly."

"No," she whispered.

"I don't blame you for questioning me, because I've been an idiot. I convinced myself that there was no way you could really love me."

"But that's—"

She stopped when he pressed his finger to her lips. "Just

let me get this out because it's not easy for me to admit some things."

With a nod, she said, "Okay."

He clenched his jaw, then began. "My parents were really bad people, really bad. They taught me some hard lessons early on. I'd rather not get into the specifics, but one of the luckiest days of my life was when Sally took me in. But even though she's a fantastic mother and I owe her everything, those first ugly memories lingered."

She put her hand on his knee for her own comfort as well as his, but didn't say anything.

"Because of those old memories," he continued, "I decided a long time ago that I would never really matter to anyone, you know? So I just made up my mind that I would never fall in love. That way, nobody could ever get close enough to hurt me."

"Oh, Brandon."

"It took your leaving for me to realize just how much I wanted to matter to you," he said. "I was blown away when you told me you were in love with me. At first, I couldn't make myself believe it. It was too...*important,* you know?"

"Yes, I know."

He covered her hand with his. "To be honest, it scared the hell out of me. But I want to be important to you, Kelly. I want you to love me, because I'm so in love with you. My heart is empty when you're not around. I can't really live without you in my life."

A tear fell from her eye and Brandon ran his thumb along her cheek to catch the next one. "Please, Kelly. Please put me out of my misery and tell me you still love me."

"Of course I still love you, Brandon," she said. "I love you with all my heart."

"Marry me?" he asked, as he touched her face with both

of his hands. "I want to spend the rest of my life showing you how much I love you."

"Yes, I'll marry you."

"I love you so much."

"Then will you kiss me, please?"

Holding back a smile, he said, "I'm not sure I remember how. Maybe you'd better show me."

She laughed and wrapped her arms around him. "Practice makes perfect."

His laughter joined hers. "Then we'd better get started."

Joy swept through her as he enfolded her in his arms and kissed her with all the love that was overflowing in his heart for her alone. And it was perfect.

Epilogue

Two years later

Midsummer along the central California coast meant warm days and balmy nights and Brandon Duke couldn't think of a better reason to throw a party. Unless it was also a surprise party celebrating his mother's birthday.

As he walked the perimeter of the backyard where family and friends were gathered, Brandon soaked up the sights and sounds of the party. He couldn't help smiling as he realized just how different his and his brothers' lives were now than they had been just a few short years ago.

Back then, this would've been a stylish cocktail party with subdued conversations. Instead, there were sudden bursts of laughter and splashing around the pool. He grinned as he caught a flash of his mom's shocking pink Capri pants that made her look like a teenager. The scents of an ocean breeze and suntan lotion blended with barbecued chicken and ice-cold lemonade.

At that moment, from across the patio, he caught Kelly's eye and felt the fierce punch of joy he always experienced when he gazed upon his beautiful wife. He watched with pride and love as she stroked her stomach where their unborn child, a baby boy, waited patiently to be born. Kelly had changed everything in his life for the better and was just days away from making him a father. Brandon knew without a doubt that with Kelly by his side, he could face any obstacle, conquer any fear. Their future was rosy indeed.

And even though his mother had denied it a thousand times, Brandon was positive she'd had something to do with bringing the two of them together. He would have to thank her some day.

Cameron came up behind him and slapped Brandon on the shoulder. "Great party, man. I think Mom was really surprised."

"For a minute there, I thought she stopped breathing," Brandon admitted, shaking his head.

"Yeah, then she burst into tears." Cameron laughed. "It was perfect."

They both glanced over and Cameron grinned as his son Jake loudly explained to his baby sister Samantha how to race a dump truck on the brick path surrounding the house. In the pool, their little cousin T.J. bobbed confidently in his proud father Adam's arms. Adam continued to insist to whoever would listen that his boy would be competing as an Olympic swimmer any day now.

"Hey, thanks for the invite, Brandon."

Brandon whirled around and saw his cousin, Aidan, popping open a bottle of beer.

"Glad you could make it," Brandon said. "It's about time

we all finally met. And it was a perfect way to surprise Mom on her birthday."

Aidan's identical twin brother, Logan, grabbed his own bottle and the two men joined Brandon and Cameron to survey the activity.

"You have a terrific family," Logan said, smiling his approval.

"Thanks," Cameron said jovially. "We're happy you guys are a part of it."

"It's all because of your mom," Aidan said, chuckling. "She shocked the hell out of Dad when she first called him. He'd been trying to track down his brother Bill for years, but when their orphanage burned down, the records were lost and he finally gave up trying."

Brandon shook his head as he thought of that fateful fire. Sally's husband Bill and his brother Tom were adopted by different families and lost touch with each other. If not for Sally Duke and her stubborn refusal to give up, the Duke brothers might never have met their cousins.

"It almost broke Sally's heart when she heard about the fire," Cameron said. "But Mom is nothing if not tenacious. Once she got the hang of Google and started searching through every bit of information she could find, it was inevitable that she would track you guys down."

"We're thankful that she did," Logan said. "Dad was over the moon about finally getting to meet all of you."

The four cousins stared across the covered patio at Sally and the tall, good-looking older man standing next to her. This was Tom, her deceased husband Bill's brother.

Brandon peered more closely and couldn't help but notice the goofy grin on Tom's face as he gazed down at Sally. He turned and frowned at Logan. "Your father's a widower, right?"

"Yeah, and your mom is a widow," Logan said with a speculative look. "What the hell?"

Adam wrapped a towel around his waist and walked over to grab a bottle of beer before joining his brothers and cousins. After taking a healthy sip of his drink, he jutted his chin in the direction of Sally and Tom, then looked at Brandon and Cameron. "They seem to be enjoying themselves."

"Yeah, we were just noticing that," Aidan said.

Cameron scratched at his beard thoughtfully. "Not sure what to think yet."

Brandon took a long, reflective pull of his beer. "Maybe this family isn't quite finished with matchmaking after all."

* * * * *

COMING NEXT MONTH

Available September 13, 2011

You can find more information on upcoming Harlequin® titles, free excerpts and more at
www.HarlequinInsideRomance.com.

HDCNM0811

REQUEST YOUR FREE BOOKS!
2 FREE NOVELS PLUS 2 FREE GIFTS!

ALWAYS POWERFUL, PASSIONATE AND PROVOCATIVE

YES! Please send me 2 FREE Harlequin Desire® novels and my 2 FREE gifts (gifts are worth about $10). After receiving them, if I don't wish to receive any more books, I can return the shipping statement marked "cancel." If I don't cancel, I will receive 6 brand-new novels every month and be billed just $4.30 per book in the U.S. or $4.99 per book in Canada. That's a saving of at least 14% off the cover price! It's quite a bargain! Shipping and handling is just 50¢ per book in the U.S. and 75¢ per book in Canada.* I understand that accepting the 2 free books and gifts places me under no obligation to buy anything. I can always return a shipment and cancel at any time. Even if I never buy another book, the two free books and gifts are mine to keep forever.

225/326 HDN FEF3

Name _____ (PLEASE PRINT)

Address _____ Apt. #

City _____ State/Prov. _____ Zip/Postal Code

Signature (if under 18, a parent or guardian must sign)

Mail to the **Reader Service:**
IN U.S.A.: P.O. Box 1867, Buffalo, NY 14240-1867
IN CANADA: P.O. Box 609, Fort Erie, Ontario L2A 5X3

Not valid for current subscribers to Harlequin Desire books.

Want to try two free books from another line?
Call 1-800-873-8635 or visit www.ReaderService.com.

* Terms and prices subject to change without notice. Prices do not include applicable taxes. Sales tax applicable in N.Y. Canadian residents will be charged applicable taxes. Offer not valid in Quebec. This offer is limited to one order per household. All orders subject to credit approval. Credit or debit balances in a customer's account(s) may be offset by any other outstanding balance owed by or to the customer. Please allow 4 to 6 weeks for delivery. Offer available while quantities last.

Your Privacy—The Reader Service is committed to protecting your privacy. Our Privacy Policy is available online at www.ReaderService.com or upon request from the Reader Service.

We make a portion of our mailing list available to reputable third parties that offer products we believe may interest you. If you prefer that we not exchange your name with third parties, or if you wish to clarify or modify your communication preferences, please visit us at www.ReaderService.com/consumerschoice or write to us at Reader Service Preference Service, P.O. Box 9062, Buffalo, NY 14269. Include your complete name and address.

HDES11B

Rafael de Luca had been in bad situations before. A crowded ballroom could never make him sweat.

These people would never know that he had no memory of any of them.

He surveyed the party with grim tolerance, searching for the source of his unease.

At first his gaze flickered past her, but he yanked his attention back to a woman across the room. Her stare bored holes through him. Unflinching and steady, even when his eyes locked with hers.

Petite, even in heels, she had a creamy olive complexion. A wealth of inky-black curls cascaded over her shoulders and her eyes were equally dark.

She looked at him as if she'd already judged him and found him lacking. He'd never seen her before in his life. Or had he?

He cursed the gaping hole in his memory. He'd been diagnosed with selective amnesia after his accident four months ago. Which seemed like complete and utter bull. No one got amnesia except hysterical women in bad soap operas.

With a smile, he disengaged himself from the group

around him and made his way to the mystery woman.

She wasn't coy. She stared straight at him as he approached, her chin thrust upward in defiance.

"Excuse me, but have we met?" he asked in his smoothest voice.

His gaze moved over the generous swell of her breasts pushed up by the empire waist of her black cocktail dress.

When he glanced back up at her face, he saw fury in her eyes.

"Have we *met?*" Her voice was barely a whisper, but he felt each word like the crack of a whip.

Before he could process her response, she nailed him with a right hook. He stumbled back, holding his nose.

One of his guards stepped between Rafe and the woman, accidentally sending her to one knee. Her hand flew to the folds of her dress.

It was then, as she cupped her belly, that the realization hit him. She was pregnant.

Her eyes flashing, she turned and ran down the marble hallway.

Rafael ran after her. He burst from the hotel lobby, and saw two shoes sparkling in the moonlight, twinkling at him.

He blew out his breath in frustration and then shoved the pair of sparkly, ultrafeminine heels at his head of security.

"Find the woman who wore these shoes."

Will Rafael find his mystery woman?
Find out in Maya Banks's passionate new novel
ENTICED BY HIS FORGOTTEN LOVER
Available September 2011 from Harlequin® Desire®!

Harlequin Desire

ALWAYS POWERFUL, PASSIONATE AND PROVOCATIVE.

**NEW YORK TIMES AND USA TODAY
BESTSELLING AUTHOR**

MAYA BANKS

**BRINGS YOU THE FIRST STORY
IN A BRAND-NEW MINISERIES**

PASSION & PREGNANCY
*When irresistible tycoons
face the consequences of temptation.*

ENTICED BY HIS
FORGOTTEN LOVER

A bout of amnesia…a mysterious woman
he can't resist…a pregnancy shocker.

When Rafael de Luca's memory comes
crashing back, it will change everything.

*Available September
wherever books are sold.*

www.Harlequin.com

SD73120R

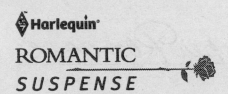

Harlequin

ROMANTIC
SUSPENSE

NEW YORK TIMES BESTSELLING AUTHOR
RACHEL LEE

The Rescue Pilot

Time is running out...

Desperate to help her ailing sister, Rory is determined
to get Cait the necessary treatment to help her fight
a devastating disease. A cross-country trip turns into
a fight for survival in more ways than one when their plane
encounters trouble. Can Rory trust pilot Chase Dakota
with their lives, and possibly her heart?

**Look for this heart-stopping romance in September
from *New York Times* bestselling author Rachel Lee
and Harlequin Romantic Suspense!**

Conard County THE NEXT GENERATION

Available in September wherever books are sold!

www.Harlequin.com.

RSRL27741

Love and family secrets collide in
a powerful new trilogy from

Linda Warren

Blood is thicker than oil

Coming August 9, 2011.

The Texan's Secret

Before Chance Hardin can join his brothers in
their new oil business, he must reveal a secret
that could tear their family apart. And his
desire for family has never been stronger, all
because of beautiful Shay Dumont.
A woman with a secret of her own....

The Texan's Bride
(October 11, 2011)

The Texan's Christmas
(December 6, 2011)